a modern fairytale

Katy Regnery

AMF

The Vixen and the Vet

(Beauty & the Beast)

Never Let You Go

(Hansel & Gretel)

Ginger's Heart

(Little Red Riding Hood)

Dark Sexy Knight

(Camelot)

Don't Speak

(The Little Mermaid)

Shear Heaven

(Rapunzel)

At First Sight

(Aladdin)

Love is Never Lost

(Rip Van Winkle)

Shear *Heaven*

a modern fairytale novella

Katy Regnery

Cover by Marianne Nowicki

Please visit my website at www.katyregnery.com
First Edition: August 2017
Second Edition: December 2017
Katy Regnery
Shear Heaven : a novella / by Katy Regnery – 1st ed.
ISBN: 978-1-944810-17-7

For Maria Raduazzo, with thanks for her help and friendship.
Abbracci e baci.

xo

CHAPTER 1

"La Contessa de Perugia requires a wash and style tomorrow, Bella. Surely we can fit her in?"

Bella blinked up at her godmother and boss, Madame Gothel, who stood beside an elegant, middle-aged woman at the reception desk of the salon.

Surely we can't, thought Bella, looking down at the already-overbooked appointment log for tomorrow. "I'm so sorry, but tomorrow is already—"

"Two o'clock?" trilled Madame Gothel, smiling at the client.

"*Sí. Perfecto. Grazie, madame.*"

"Brilliant. Add la Contessa to the schedule at two, Bella."

It occurred to her to ask, *With whom?* but she held her tongue, writing "Perugia" in tiny letters next to the four already-confirmed appointments.

Madame smiled at the contessa, gesturing with her palm to the glass doors that led to the hotel elevator. "I'm leaving for today. Let me walk you out." Looking over her shoulder, she scanned the reception area before sniffing at Bella. "Straighten up in here before locking up, Bella. I'll see you at home. Good night."

Though her shift should have ended three hours ago, Bella nodded. "Of course. Good night, Madame."

Dropping her eyes back to the appointment book, Bella stared at tomorrow's schedule in dismay. Madame Gothel's intimate, world-famous Innsbruck Salon and Spa, located on the top floor of New York's Metro Tower Hotel, was in high demand but *seriously* understaffed.

It didn't help that the last receptionist had only lasted three days before Madame had sacked her. Which meant Bella was now working double duty: as a stylist from nine to five every day and as receptionist from five to eight every evening as well. Though she didn't recall agreeing to the increased responsibilities and hours, Bella's parents had passed away four years ago, and Madame Gothel, her godmother, had taken her in when she had nowhere else to go. Besides, there was something about Madame that made refusing unthinkable. And a little terrifying.

Closing the appointment book, Bella sighed. Five appointments. Four stylists. They'd have to figure it out tomorrow. *Perhaps one of the other two o'clock appointments would cancel*, she thought, though she knew it was unlikely.

Opening the desk drawer, she grabbed the ring of salon keys, then walked over to the glass doors, squatting down to lock them. Back at the desk, she took out the Windex and a fresh rag, then got to work shining the chrome desk top, the glass doors, and the many decorative mirrors and shiny surfaces in the small reception room. She watered the plants, taking care to remove the brown leaves and throw them in the trash. As she fanned out the magazines on the end tables, enjoying the quiet, a knock on the glass doors made her jump, and she whipped around to see a man standing in the darkened lobby, his hand raised in greeting.

"Are you open?" he enunciated carefully through the glass.

She shook her head no, stepping over to the locked doors. "Sorry."

"Damn it," he muttered, his eyebrows knitting together as he stared at her.

As she drew closer, she felt her face soften as she stared through the glass into dark eyes surrounded with longer and thicker lashes than any man on earth had a right to. She guessed he was about her age—in his midtwenties—and he wore a tailored tuxedo, pressed and perfect on his tall, filled-out frame, a white rosebud tucked into the lapel.

"We reopen tomorrow morning."

"I need help now," he pressed, running a hand through his dark hair.

"I'm sorry," she said, wringing her hands together. Madame would have her head if she suddenly reopened the salon after hours without permission. "I can try to fit you in tomorrow morning at—"

"No! Please. Let me explain," he said, holding up his hands in surrender. "My sister, Valentina…she is…" He rubbed the dark beard on his chin with his thumb and forefinger.

"Your sister?" she prompted.

"She needs help getting ready."

"Oh?"

"For her engagement party"—he glanced at his watch—"which is in three-quarters of an hour." He sighed, clenching his jaw. "*Per favore*! This is…eh! *Che casino*!" *What a mess!*

She froze, the sound of her native language disarming her, making her lean forward and ask automatically, "*Posso aiutarla*?" *How can I help?*

His face, which had been fraught with consternation, softened, his lips tilting up in a slight smile as he looked down at her through the glass.

"*Parli italiano*?" *You speak Italian?*

"*Sì*," she replied. "*Sono svizzero, de Ticino*." *Yes. I'm Swiss, from Ticino.*

"*Sei lontano de casa*." *You're far away from home.* As he said this, he unfurled his fists, which were by his sides.

"*Sì*."

"*Mi aiuterai per favore, bella*?" *Will you help me, beautiful?*

Bella.

She knew that he'd only used the word as a common endearment, but hearing her name tumble from his gorgeous lips was her ultimate undoing.

What Madame didn't know wouldn't hurt her.

She nodded, kneeling down on the floor, pulling the keys from the pocket of her dark-blue denim skirt and unlocking the door. Rising slowly, she noted the shiny, stiff black leather of his shoes, the purple silk cummerbund with a repeat of golden shields, and the crisp, white shirt tucked into his trim waist. She took a deep breath and lifted her eyes to his, forcing herself not to linger on the fullness of his lips or swoon when she looked into his dark-blue eyes.

His hand reached for the door handle, and he pulled it open.

She'd been deprived of his smell from the other side of the glass, but the breath she held became painful as her heart thundered against her ribs in recognition of it: Acqua Nobile.

Exhaling softly, she breathed in through her nose, her eyes fluttering closed just for a moment as she savored the scent.

"*Signorina?*"

Blinking her eyes open, she looked up at his face, taking another deep breath. "*Sí?*"

"Do you arrange hair?"

"Hair?"

"*Capelli?*" he asked, pointing to his head.

Capelli. Her surname. She nodded at him, feeling dreamy from the combination of his ridiculous eyelashes and delicious smell and hearing her name issue from his lips yet again. "*Sí.*"

"*Stupendo,*" he said, reaching for her hand and pulling her from the glass tower. "Come with me."

***

His Serene Highness Nicolo Alessandro Lorenzo Giovanni De'Medici was not accustomed to begging for help from anyone, but his twin sister, Valentina, had stumbled into their shared hotel suite an hour ago, after being out all last night and most of today. Though he doubted very much that she'd been drinking, she smelled of *Eau d'Club*: a mixture of liquor, cigarette smoke, and sweat; her blonde hair was tangled; and her eyes were bloodshot and weary. Nico had ordered her into the shower, then left the suite, scrambling to find someone to get her in presentable condition for the engagement festivities that were starting at nine o'clock.

Racing to the elevator, Nico's plan had been to go downstairs to the concierge to ask for help, until he noticed a hotel business listing on the elevator wall, including a salon and spa within the hotel. He'd pressed the button for the thirty-second floor instead, relieved to find someone still moving around inside the dark reception area.

When she'd first turned around, he'd felt an instant jolt of heat sluice through his body.

Were he handed a brush and told to paint a picture of his "type"—of the sort of girl who attracted him more than any other—little by little, her image would appear on the canvas.

She was petite with jet-black hair and dark-brown eyes. A tight, black leotard-like top hugged her lush, rounded breasts, showcasing the creamy white skin of her chest. She wore no jewelry and very little makeup, but she needed neither in his opinion. His eyes had dropped to her tiny waist, then to the full, dark-blue skirt she wore a la Audrey Hepburn in *Roman Holiday*.

There was a country freshness to her that had only been reaffirmed with the realization that she spoke Italian with a Swiss accent. The Italian-Swiss state of Ticino sat almost entirely surrounded by Italy on the south, west, and most of the east and was known for its rivers, lakes, and farmable land. Generally regarded as less sophisticated than the rest of Switzerland, it boasted a healthy wine industry, and Nico imagined this girl, with her dark hair unbound, standing in the afternoon sunlight of a Swiss vineyard, surrounded by plump grapes, green leaves, and rich soil the approximate color of her eyes.

He still held her wrist as they entered the elevator side by side, but she pulled away from him as the chrome doors closed, taking a step to her left as he swiped his card and pressed nineteen. It was only then Nico realized that he hadn't properly introduced himself to her.

"Ah-hem," he started in English, facing her and holding out his hand. "I'm Nico De'Medici."

She turned slightly, taking his outstretched hand in her much smaller one. "De'Medici? That's a famous name in Tuscany."

He shook her hand gently. "I'm from Fiesole."

"I've visited *Villa Medici* in Florence," she said, pulling her hand away.

He grinned at her casual reference to his family's ancestral home. "Mm. Yes. They kept the name, but the castle was overtaken by the Borghese family more than two hundred years ago."

"Damn Borgheses, always stealing castles," she said lightly, chuckling softly.

She seemed fairly proper, so her comment surprised him, but he laughed along with her. "Sold, not stolen. *We* relocated to an eighteenth-century villa in the hills. Much less drafty."

"Oh, of course," she said, nodding merrily as though colluding with him. "No one wants to live in big, drafty castles today with the cost of petrol so outrageous. Villas are so much cozier."

Her tone made it clear that she didn't recognize him, but then, she wasn't actually one of his countrymen, since she was Swiss and he was Italian. Very Italian. As the only son of His Serene Highness Prince Filipe De'Medici, Nico was an Italian prince.

An Italian prince with a dwindling family fortune, he thought, thinking of the villa he'd just mentioned, which his family was on the brink of losing.

"I loved Florence," she commented with a small, wistful sigh.

"Were you only there once?" he asked.

"Oh, no. Many times. When my parents were still…" Her voice trailed off and she dropped his eyes, looking down at her little black slipper-shoes.

"Your parents?"

"We traveled a great deal in Italy," she finished softly.

He sensed that speaking about her parents bothered her, so he nudged her gently in the side with his elbow, trying to lighten the mood. "But you never met any De'Medicis or Borgheses on your travels, eh?"

"Wouldn't that be something?" she asked, her eyes brightening again as she looked up at him and grinned. "To meet a *real* Medici or Borghese?"

He tilted his head to the side. "Think so?"

She nodded. "The Italian nobility isn't nearly as famous as the British, of course. I mean, I could pick William or Harry out of a crowd, but plop an Italian prince in front of me and I'd have no idea."

"None at all," he echoed, staring at her sweet expression.

"But I still think it would be fun. You know, to meet *actual* royalty."

"Hmm." He wondered if he should reveal his identity, but he was enjoying her comments way too much to confess who he was. "Maybe you will. Someday."

The elevator dinged on the nineteenth floor, and Nico held the door for her, watching her skirt swirl softly as she stepped from the lift to the plush carpeting of the hotel's presidential level.

"I've never been on this floor," she whispered. "Only guests and 'necessary staff' have keycards."

"Well, consider yourself necessary staff tonight," he said, exiting the elevator.

Nico glanced at his watch. It was almost eight thirty and Valentina would be expected downstairs in the Grand Ballroom in exactly thirty minutes.

"Come on," he said, turning left down a wide, elegant hallway.

She followed behind him, her footsteps soft.

"I didn't catch your name," he said over his shoulder.

"It's Bella," she said. "Bella Capelli."

He stopped short and turned to look at her. "Your name means 'beautiful hair'?"

She blinked at him, then shrugged.

"Is that a joke?"

"No."

"A pseudonym? For work purposes?"

"No," she said again. "It's my real name."

"Coincidence or fate?" he asked, staring into her bright, coffee-colored eyes.

"Both?" she murmured.

"Coincidence *and* fate," he said softly, then added, "Your eyes are very beautiful too, Bella Capelli."

"*Grazie*," she murmured, her pink lips softly parted as she gazed up at him.

Not far down the hallway, they heard the sound of pottery hitting a wall and shattering to the floor, and both of them flinched, turning in the direction of the melee.

Hmm. Valentina must be out of the shower.

"*Cos'hai?*" she asked. *What was that?*

He looked at her wide eyes, then grabbed her elbow. "Valentina can be...a handful."

She didn't resist him, so he tugged her the remaining hundred feet, pulled his key card from his pocket, and flashed it in front of the reader.

"Ready, Bella Capelli?"

"For what?" she asked.

"To meet my sister."

Without giving her time to respond, he surged through the door to his suite, holding it open for her to follow.

***

The gorgeous parlor was in complete disarray.

A coffee table was resting on its side, throw pillows were lying on the floor, and a smashed coffee mug lay in pieces on the hardwood floor.

Someone was having a tantrum.

"*Vai a cagare!*" screamed Valentina, stalking out of the bedroom holding the in-room coffeemaker, a white towel wrapped around her chest and her wet hair lying limp around her shoulders. She spied Nico and Bella by the suite door. "*Chi é lei?*"

Who is she? she demanded of Nico, narrowing her eyes and staring daggers at Bella.

"This is Bella," he said. "*Lavora al parrucchiere dell'hotel.*" *She works in the hotel salon.*

"You are...hair stylist?" asked Valentina in heavily accented English.

"Yes," said Bella, flicking an uneasy glance at the coffeemaker.

Valentina sighed with annoyance. "What *ees* your specialty?"

Bella turned her head slightly, showing the intricate braids woven into a complicated bun on the base of her neck. "I did this without a mirror. Do you like it?"

"*Eet's* okay," she said, fighting to look unimpressed. She lifted her chin, looking down her nose at Bella. "Understand, stylist-girl, I need hair for princess."

She scoffed lightly. *Someone* has a high opinion of herself.

Bella gestured to the desk and chair to her right, then reached for the poor coffeemaker. "Why don't you give this to me and take a seat over there? We'll get started."

Valentina frowned at the machine in Bella's arms. "*That* is broken...and I *need* coffee."

Turning away as Valentina sauntered over to the desk, Bella reached down to right the upended coffee table and placed the troublesome coffeemaker on it. She lifted her eyes to Nico. "Could you ask room service to send up some coffee?"

"Of course," he said, cocking his head to the side. "You know, you're very calming. You're good with her."

Bella offered him a slight smile, then glanced at his sister, who plopped down in the desk chair with an irritated sigh. "Does *her highness* have a brush?"

"Her *Serene* Highness," said Nico, winking at her, "has a brush in the bathroom. I will get it for you and take care of the coffee."

Her *serene* highness. *Ha! As if!*

Bella grinned at his joke before crossing the room to stand behind Valentina. She gathered the damp hair in her hands, running her fingers through it. "You have lovely hair."

"*Grazie*," answered Valentina, looking at herself in the mirror over the desk. Her eyes were sad. Heartsick, even.

"We'll make it look very beautiful," said Bella, hoping to make her feel better. "Don't worry."

Valentina searched Bella's eyes in the mirror, then looked at herself. "Are you…married, *signorina*?"

"No, I'm not," answered Bella, shaking her head and continuing the soothing movement of her fingers through Valentina's long, blonde hair. "I've just turned twenty-two. I don't know if I'm ready yet."

"I'm nearly twenty-seven," said Valentina, taking a deep breath and closing her eyes, "and I don't know if I am either."

"Are you planning to get married?" asked Bella.

"*Sí*," answered Valentina. "Next weekend."

Bella sectioned the hair, gently untangling each of the smaller sections and letting the air remove some of the moisture as she gently pulled the unruly strands straight. "Do you think you'll be ready by then?"

Valentina took a deep breath and sighed. "I doubt it."

"Can you postpone?"

"The wedding? No. *Assolutamente fuori discussione.*" *It's out of the question.*

"Do you love him?"

"I don't"—Valentina's voice trailed off as Bella moved to another section of hair—"*know* him."

Bella's bottom lip slipped between her teeth, as it often did when she was faced with a puzzling circumstance. Why in the world would you marry someone—bind your life to someone—you didn't love?

Not that she knew very much about love personally, but her parents had loved each other very much, and that was all Bella needed to know. She wanted a marriage like theirs or none at all.

"Do you want to talk about it?" asked Bella.

"No." Valentina sighed again, her eyes tightly closed. "Be silent, stylist-girl. Do my hair. Let me to relax."

Honestly, thought Bella, swallowing a scoff but rolling her eyes at her reflection in the mirror. Being rich didn't entitle one to act like such a spoiled brat.

There was a knock on the suite door, and Nico appeared from the bedroom to answer it. A waiter that Bella recognized from the kitchen entered the room with a linen-covered tray that bore a silver coffee service and two teacups.

"Hey, Bella," he said, winking at her as he placed the tray on the coffee table.

She nodded at him. "Hi, Marco."

"You're working late." Marco looked up at Nico. "Shall I pour, sir?"

Nico's eyes, which tracked the distance between Bella and Marco, were slightly narrowed. "No, thanks. That'll be all."

He pulled his wallet from his back pocket, took out what appeared to be a twenty-dollar bill, and offered it to Marco.

Marco took it with a grin. "If you need anything else, sir, please let me know."

Nico nodded at him, gesturing to the door, then turned to the coffee service, pouring a cup and bringing it over to his sister. He placed it on the desk before her.

"*Bevi,* Tina." *Drink.*

"*Lasciami in pace,*" mumbled Valentina. *Leave me alone.*

He shrugged, placing his sister's brush on the desk and looking at Bella in the mirror. "Do you want some coffee?"

Bella had assumed the second cup was for him. "Don't *you* want some?"

He shook his head, glancing at the tray, then back at her. "No. But I thought you might."

Touched by his unnecessary thoughtfulness, she smiled at him. "I'd love a cup. Thank you."

***

As Nico returned to the coffeepot, he glanced back to see Bella raise her arms and reach behind her neck. One by one, she plucked pin after pin from her hair, placing them into a quickly growing pile on the desk where Valentina sat in quiet misery. Holding the coffeepot, Nico stood frozen, watching in rapt fascination as her mane of black waves was freed, the longest of the tresses extending well past her waist. As she pulled the final pin, she shook her head back and forth, and he realized that her hair was so long, it tumbled in waves past her shoulders, ending just south of her ass.

His mind processed this new information to the lowest common denominator, imagining what she'd look like completely naked except for that dark hair falling over her creamy white shoulders, covering her breasts as she rode him, his hands holding her hips as she—

Whoa.

Wait.

He blinked rapidly, looking back into the mirror, where he found her staring at him, only this time, he was the one with wide eyes and flushed cheeks, his trousers just starting to tent as he locked his eyes on hers.

"Nico, get my black Chanel dress out of the closet? And my light-pink Manolo Blahniks? They have a black buckle."

Spurred into action by his sister's request, he reached for the remaining coffee cup, poured her coffee, and crossed the room to place it on the desk. "Uh, yeah. Yeah. I'll just…"

Avoiding Bella's eyes, he turned briskly and headed to Tina's room, quickly finding the items she needed and laying them out on her bed. Her black dress looked so stark and small against the light-blue satin duvet; it was a reminder to him that she'd be growing out of it very soon.

He winced as he reentered the living room.

"You don't *have* to marry him, Tina."

"Yes, I do I have to marry *someone*," she said.

"It doesn't have to be him."

"What difference does it make?" asked Valentina in Italian, a note of desperation squeezing Nico's heart.

"How can you build a life with him? You won't reconsider your options, *sorellina*?"

"Lui è ricco." He's rich. She looked up at her brother meaningfully, and his jaw ticked with quiet anger. He and Valentina hadn't squandered the family fortune, and yet they were the ones expected to recover it through loveless marriages. It made him furious.

"*Vorrei che le cose erano diverse*," he finally said softly. *I wish things were different.*

Valentina shrugged, then sniffled softly, nodding at her reflection, which was more refined and elegant with every flick and twist of Bella's nimble fingers.

"It's all arranged," she said, practicing her English. "Leave it be, Nico. *Va bene.*"

Looking up from his sister, he found Bella's brown eyes searching for his in the mirror, a myriad of questions brightening them. Because discussing his twin sister's shame wasn't something that interested Nico, he raised his chin and asked, "Do you have everything you need? We're running out of time."

The softness in her face instantly tightened, and she nodded. "I'll be finished in a moment."

"What else do you need, Tina?" he asked his sister.

"A new life?" she quipped.

"All done," said Bella, twisting a final piece of hair into the elegant arrangement and securing it with the final pin from the desk.

Valentina opened her eyes and stood up, checking out Bella's quick work. Though she still wore a towel, she had a regal coronet on her head now, and while she didn't exactly look the picture of a blushing bride-to-be, it was certainly an improvement on the mess she'd been when she'd first returned to the hotel suite an hour ago.

"Okay," she said softly, nodding at her reflection. She turned to Bella, offering the hotel stylist a sad smile. "*Grazie.*"

"*Prego*," answered Bella, her eyes sympathetic.

Valentina headed to her room to get ready, closing the door behind her, and Nico checked his watch again. They'd only be a few minutes late if she was quick.

Bella reached down to the desk to gather the leftover pins into her palm, then pivoted to face Nico. "Was there anything else?"

He looked closely at her—at her dark hair tumbling in waves around her shoulders, her dark eyes and soft lips. She'd saved his ass tonight—and his sister's too. "I owe you."

She grinned at him, shaking her head and pushing the chair back into the desk. "No, you don't. It only took a few minutes."

She was kind. And decent. And she'd made him laugh.

After a few days in this fast-paced, grabby, grimy city, she was a breath of fresh air, and he wished he could get to know her better.

"Listen," he said, taking a step toward her, words he didn't expect or anticipate suddenly falling from his lips, "I'm going to be in town for another week. How would you feel about—"

Valentina's bedroom door opened, and she stepped into the living room, looking every bit the young princess. She approached Bella, holding out a small tiara. "Will you help me?"

"Of course," said Bella, taking the diamond tiara from her. She pressed it carefully into the intricate hairstyle, using two of the pins clasped in her hand to secure it. Then she stepped back and smiled. "You look beautiful, *signorina*. Like a princess."

"Yes. Yes." Valentina sighed heavily, then turned to Nico. "*Andiamo*?"

"*Sí*," he said, holding out his hand to her and clasping it firmly within his. Turning to Bella, he cocked his head to the side, trying to feel relieved that his impetuous almost-offer to take her out to dinner had been diverted. "You saved the day. I don't know how to thank you enough. Please bill us."

"*Non*," she said, shaking her head, smiling at him sweetly. "*Senza alcun costo, signor*."

No charge.

Ignoring the urge to drop his sister's hand and pull this strange little Swiss girl into his arms, he nodded at her in thanks, promising himself to figure out a way to repay her kindness to them.

"*Grazie*, Bella Capelli," he said, forcing himself not to rake his eyes down her body as Valentina tugged him toward the door.

"*Prego*, Nico De'Medici," she said softly, nodding at him and his sister in farewell as they slipped through the door, leaving her behind.

CHAPTER 2

"Bellllla!" trilled Madame Gothel as Bella pulled the front door to the apartment closed and locked it. "Is that youuuuuu?"

Bella rolled her eyes toward the ceiling. *Dio dammi la forza. God give me strength*, she thought, crossing herself.

"*Sí, Madrina.*" *Yes, Godmother.*

"English, pleeeeease," her godmother reminded her, rounding the corner of the living room in a pink silk bathrobe, her long, dark hair wound up in a scarf and her face covered with an aqua-colored masque. "What took so long? Did you lock up?"

Bella offered her boss/godmother a small smile, quickly deciding to keep her dealings with the De'Medici twins to herself. "*Sí*...uh, yes."

"Excellent," said her godmother, putting her arm around Bella's small shoulders. "Whatever would I dooooo without you?"

You did just fine until I got here, she thought, letting herself be ushered into the living room, which her godmother preferred to call "the Gran Salon."

Helga Gothel and Bella's mother, Karin Schmidt, had been girlhood friends, growing up in the same historic German-Swiss village of Brig, not far from the Italian border. In primary school and secondary school, the girls and Bella's father, Giorgio Capelli, had been inseparable. When they turned eighteen, Giorgio had proposed to Karin, and Helga had decided to study abroad in America.

With the help of their parents, Karin and Giorgio had purchased and tended a small vineyard and grotto—a rustic, family-run restaurant—making local wines and serving good

Swiss-Italian fare. Helga, on the other hand, had used her parents' money to open a small but prosperous hair salon in Brooklyn, New York, that eventually turned into six salons in Manhattan. When she met Klaus Ingraham, partial owner of the New York Metro Tower Hotel, she was thirty to his fifty-six, but he gave her what she'd wanted from the very beginning: a chance to own and operate the premiere hotel salon and spa in New York City—the Innsbruck.

Klaus had passed away in short order, leaving his young bride a penthouse apartment, the salon, and his share of the hotel.

Unbeknown to Helga, the Capellis had named her Bella's legal guardian, and when Karin and Giorgio died in a train crash when Bella was only seventeen, Helga had been compelled to offer Bella a place to live. So Bella had moved into her godmother's luxurious penthouse on the thirtieth floor of the hotel...

...and while she grieved the terrible loss of her beloved parents, she became a combination of Madame's right-hand gal, student, apprentice, companion, and the child she'd never had.

But Bella had quickly learned that Helga and Karin had very different ideas about motherhood, and where Bella's own mother had been warm and loving, encouraging her daughter to make her own path in the world, Helga was domineering and manipulative, expecting Bella to work very long hours and dedicate her life wholly to the Innsbruck and to Helga's comfort. With her own mother, Bella had been encouraged to chase her dreams; with Madame, Bella felt like a prisoner in a velvet-padded cell.

But with her passport and green card locked up in her godmother's desk for "safekeeping," it wasn't as if she could just grab them and leave. And anyway, where would she go? Madame didn't pay her a salary; Bella lived rent-free with her godmother and was, for all intents and purposes, her daughter. She was given a credit card for clothes and toiletries and was fed and sheltered in luxury. And yet...with no real money of her own and no identification, Bella was trapped.

Trapped in a beautiful place and being taught a valuable trade, she reminded herself, trying to be grateful. One day, Bella believed she would own and operate the Innsbruck herself. Certainly then she'd be able to do whatever and go wherever she pleased.

"Bella, daaaaaarling," said Madame, leading her goddaughter to the sofa by the elbow and forcing her to sit down beside her, "we must talk briefly, my love, about your manner with the conteeeeeeessa this evening."

Briefly? Ha.

"At the Innsbruck," started Madame pedantically with an edge in her voice, "we offer luxury. We cater to a certain kind of clientele. We cannot afford to make European royalty feel unwanted, dearest. Do you understand?"

"Of course, *Madrina*, but—"

"There are no buts, Bella," said Madame, her eyes narrowing to irritated slits. "You will rearrange the appointments tomorrow so that the Countess of Perugia is with Joaquin at two o'clock sharp."

"And Mrs. Carnegie, who is already booked with him…?" she asked, daring to question her boss.

Madame raised her chin, her eyes narrowing further, her lips pursing. "Figure it out."

Bella's shoulders slumped. *How* was she was supposed to figure it out? How was she supposed to have Joaquin service two clients at once? Looking into her godmother's steel-gray eyes, Bella felt an overwhelming wave of longing for her mother's kind brown eyes and blinked back a sudden burn of tears.

"Oh, Bella, you look absolutely exhausted," said Madame, pushing Bella's long, black hair behind her shoulder. "After you straighten up here, you simply muuuuuuust go to bed."

Though Bella's aunt had the hotel maid staff at their disposal, Madame felt that it was good discipline for Bella to "pitch in" at home too. So after her shift at the salon each day, she was expected to "straighten up" at home…which meant wiping down the kitchen counters; collecting the garbage and taking it to the incinerator; running the vacuum over the carpets in the living room, dining room and den; and giving the three penthouse bathrooms a quick but thorough clean.

"Yes, *Madrina*."

Madame toyed with a strand of Bella's hair, running it through her fingers, the shiny, blood red of her lacquered nails a striking contrast against the black tresses. "This hair is probably worth thousands of dollars."

"Really?"

"Mmmm. Beautiful, black, virgin hair. So like Giorgio's."

Bella's face softened, and she looked up at Madame, hoping for a few kind words about her parents. "I miss them so much."

Madame dropped the hair suddenly, offering her charge a brittle smile. "This mask is dry. I must rinse it off. Turn off the lights when you're finished, dear? And get some sleeeeeeeeep, dearest. You look almost haggard. Tsk, tsk, tsk. What will our clients think? You must take better caaaaaaare of yourself."

"Yes, *Madrina*."

Her godmother patted her cheek gently, then rose from the couch, sauntering across the living room and down the hallway to her bedroom suite, leaving Bella alone.

***

I need air.

Nico stepped onto the elevator, staring at the panel of buttons for a second before deciding to try his luck with the roof instead of the lobby. Certainly, in the lobby, there'd be more American heiresses with visions of tiaras on their heads, far more in love with the idea of marrying a prince than actually getting to know him.

He watched the numbers over the door light up, going higher and higher. With any luck, there'd be a door that led to the roof on the thirty-third floor, and he'd have a few minutes of quiet before retiring to bed. Alone.

A bell dinged on his arrival at the top floor, and he exited the elevator onto a dimly lit, quiet lobby. Directly across from him was a long, gilt-framed mirror, and he stared at his reflection as the chrome doors closed behind him.

He hated what was happening to Tina downstairs, having to put on a happy face and pretend she was fine with marrying an American businessman she barely knew and didn't love. But having a child out of wedlock, while *normale* for most other twentysomethings in Europe, was absolutely unthinkable for most European royalty.

Unless you lived in Monaco, he thought with a grimace.

Tina's fiancé, Steve Trainor, whom Nico had only met for the first time tonight, was someone their father had suggested as a suitor. Fifteen years older than Tina, and richer than Midas, he owned one of the largest shipping companies in America. A forty-one year old bachelor with impeccable style, rumors about his sexuality had plagued him for the past decade. Marrying Tina would solve two big problems for Steve: one, it would upgrade his landside connections in Genoa, Italy, the second-largest shipping port in the country, but two, it would put to rest whispers of Steve's homosexuality, something that had apparently bothered him for years.

But the casualty of this arrangement would certainly be Tina.

With such a huge age gap and no promise of compatibility, she would be bound in marriage to someone she didn't know and couldn't love. But she'd be paid well for it: a generous allowance while they were married and a fifty million dollar settlement at the end of ten years. One of Steve's major conditions had been Tina's promise to remain married to him for a decade…which meant that Tina, his beloved twin, would be trapped with Steve until she was in her late-thirties—all so that the De'Medici name wouldn't have the public blight of a bastard, and money to refill its coffers. It simply seemed too high a price for one person to pay. But Tina had adamantly refused to share the name of her lover, which had left Nico's hands tied, unable to help her.

He closed his eyes and sighed, turning away from the mirror and starting left down the hallway. He saw a nondescript door at the end with a sign that read, "Roof Access. Hotel Personnel Only."

To hell with that. He felt in his pocket for his Swiss army knife. If he had to, he'd pick the lock for a few minutes of fresh air and solitude.

But as luck would have it, he didn't have to pick anything. As he approached, he could see that there was something lodged in the door, holding it open. Looking closely, he realized that it was a comb. A black plastic hair comb. He plucked it from its spot, carefully replacing it as soon as he was on the other side and wondering who'd put it there. The face of the beautiful hair stylist from earlier tonight flitted through his mind.

Bella Capelli.

Although he'd been seeking quiet, he certainly wouldn't mind running into her again. She'd been an oasis of calm in an otherwise chaotic evening, agreeing to help him and speaking his native language with her charming, country accent. Even joking with him about meeting royalty one day, there was still nothing wheedling or conniving about her. She was a figurative breath of fresh air, and Nico, unable to stop thinking about her for the remainder of the evening, found himself longing for more, no matter how ill advised.

Taking the dingy stairs two at a time, he opened the door to the roof and stepped outside, careful not to let the door slam shut behind him.

He wasn't surprised to find that there was no pool or bar on this rooftop—it was a functional space with air conditioning vents and satellite dishes mounted along a low balustrade made of cement. It had been paved, however, and was well maintained, and as Nico turned to the left, rounding the stairway, he saw a lone woman several yards away sitting at a picnic table, her elbows propped up and the white light of a cell phone screen backlighting her head.

"Hello!" he called out, not wanting to frighten her with his sudden presence.

She whipped her head around, several feet of long black hair swishing to the side. "Who's there?"

"I'm a hotel guest," he said, approaching slowly, coming into the moonlight as he moved away from the stairway. "It's...Bella, right?"

She nodded.

"I'm Nico De'Medici. Remember? We met earlier."

Her shoulders, which he realized had been up around her ears, relaxed, and she nodded again. "Of course. *Buona sera, signor.*"

"*Buona sera, signorina,*" he said, dropping a glance to her cell phone. "I'm interrupting you."

"You are," she said, but she softened the words by grinning up at him as she placed the phone on the table. "But I don't mind."

He felt his smile swell before he could stop it. "It's a beautiful night."

"Yes, it is," she said, offering him a small, sweet smile of her own, "and you've found my secret hiding place, though hotel guests are really not allowed up here."

"If you don't tell, I won't." He gestured to the rickety table. "May I join you?"

"Of course," she said, opening her palm to indicate that the bench across from her was free.

Unbuttoning his tuxedo jacket, he shrugged out of it, laying it across the wooden bench before sitting down. As he reached for his left cuff link, removing it to roll up his sleeve, he looked at her. "It's good to see you again, Bella Capelli."

If it wasn't so dark, he was sure he would have seen her blush.

"How is your sister?" she asked. "Valentina?"

Nico's smile faded as he placed the second cuff link on the table and rolled up his right sleeve. "Bearing up."

"Can I ask you a question?"

"Go for it," he said, propping his elbows on the table.

"Why is she marrying someone she doesn't love?"

He clenched his jaw reflexively. "Did she say that?"

Bella nodded. "She did. Well, actually she said that she doesn't *know* him…and she looked—well, honestly—miserable. I'm just—I guess I don't understand."

"What don't you understand?"

"There's only one reason to marry," she said simply.

"And that is…?"

"Love," she said, holding his eyes so earnestly, his heart clutched. She was so guileless, so sincere and straightforward, he wished he could see the world through her brown eyes instead of his own far-more-jaded blue.

"That is the *best* reason," he said gently. Somewhat reluctant to shatter her romantic notions about marriage, he offered her a sad smile to cushion the blow of his next words. "But there are other reasons, of course."

"How can there be? Pledging to love, honor, and cherish someone would be so much easier if it was actually true."

Nico leaned back a little. It wasn't his nature to talk about his sister to someone he barely knew. In fact, most of their lives, he and Tina had been counseled not to ever talk about personal matters with someone whose loyalty hadn't been trusted and found strong.

But this girl, sitting in the moonlight with her dark hair and gentle questions, seemed so genuine, he couldn't help unburdening himself.

"*Lei é incinta*," he said softly. "The baby's coming this winter."

"Oh," murmured Bella, her delectable lips open in a perfect *O*. "Oh, I see. An…*unplanned* pregnancy. They didn't mean to—"

"Her fiancé isn't the father."

"Oh!"

If her eyes got any wider, they'd take up her whole face, he thought, his lips twitching in unexpected merriment.

"Why...um, I mean, that is—why isn't she marrying the baby's father?"

Nico's mood instantly soured. "She *would* be...if she'd tell me who it was."

Bella winced, then nodded. "She's keeping him a secret? Do you have any idea who it might be?"

Sighing, he shook his head. "Tina's an independent woman. Her own job. Her own apartment. Her own friends. She works in Rome. I love her, but I don't see her that often. She came home when she found out she was in trouble."

"You're Catholic?"

He nodded. "Very."

She held his eyes, but he could almost feel the gears in her head shifting and whirring; he knew that she was thinking carefully about the situation, and somehow he knew that she was trying to find the good in it. When her lips tipped up and her eyes brightened, he held his breath.

"Then she *is* marrying for love, after all," said Bella, reaching across the table to take his hands in hers.

"What do you mean?" he asked, letting her delicate fingers wrap around his hands and hold them.

Her smile grew, and she squeezed his fingers. "For the love of her child."

For the love of her child.

It was so simple, yet so enormous.

So obvious, yet so pure.

Tina could have quietly gotten rid of the child, of course, but she'd chosen not to. She'd chosen to have it. She'd chosen to marry someone she barely knew so that her child would have a name and respectability. Bella was right. Tina *was* marrying for love.

Tears pricked his eyes, and he blinked them, his bottom lip slipping between his teeth as he adjusted his fingers to lace through hers. When his lungs started burning, he took a deep breath, then released it, feeling less in knots than he'd felt for three weeks.

"Where did you come from?" he asked softly, thinking, *From heaven.*

"Ticino," she answered, cocking her head to the side and grinning at him.

"Let me take you out for dinner tomorrow night."

Looking down at their hands as though she'd just realized they were clasped together, she pulled hers away and folded them on the edge of the table, just in front of her breasts. It was a defensive move, and he didn't like it.

"I work very late hours on Saturday."

"Sunday then?"

She shook her head. "I reconcile the books on Sunday nights."

"Monday."

"I deep clean the salon and spa."

"Tuesday?"

"Work."

"Wednesday, then."

"I take a class at City College," she said, swinging her legs over the bench as though preparing to leave.

"Thursday?" he cried, standing from his seat.

She stood as well, then turned to face him, crossing her arms over her chest.

"I'm busy," she said, her wistful smile filled with such quiet longing, it tightened his chest and hurt his heart.

Why did she have to work so hard? Weren't there maids here at the hotel to deep clean the facilities? Why was she stuck doing it?

Was it just an excuse so that she didn't have to go out with him?

No. He didn't believe that. They had just enjoyed talking to one another. He was certain of it.

Besides, his debt to her was mounting: first, she'd come to Tina's rescue earlier, and now, she'd somehow found the perfect way to comfort him about his sister's marriage.

And yet, while she was so busy being his savior, he sensed that her life—full of work without a moment for fun—wasn't at all what she wanted and certainly wasn't at all what she deserved.

She lifted her arm and swept it from one side of her body to the other. "Aren't the lights magnificent?"

Nico glanced over his shoulder. It looked like every other major city at night—no different, no better.

"Someday," she said. "Someday I'm going to get to see this big city."

"Friday?" he murmured urgently. "Please."

"I'm sorry." She took a deep breath and smiled gently at him. "Good night, Nico De'Medici. *Buona sera.*"

He watched her turn and walk away, wondering if he should try to stop her, then deciding against it. He'd figure out another way to see her.

"Good night, Bella," he called to her back, missing her already. "*Buona sera, angelo dolce.*"

Good night, sweet angel.

***

How tempted she'd been to say yes to handsome Nico last night in the moonlight, but Madame Gothel strictly forbade Bella to date hotel guests. It was the first and most important of her godmother's many rules, and Bella simply didn't have the courage to break it. Not for a man who'd be gone in a week.

Before he'd interrupted her, she'd been looking at pictures of her parents in their vineyard, at their restaurant, on vacation in Milan, Florence, and Rome. She'd been feeling very melancholy, in fact, before he'd arrived. He had no idea how much his company had been needed and how much his invitation to dinner flattered her. She had no idea what he did for a living, though he had the polished look of a banker or lawyer and was staying on the most expensive floor of the hotel.

What fun we could have for a week, she thought longingly but banished the idea quickly. And then what? If Madame found out, she'd throw Bella out of the hotel. Penniless. Homeless. Heartbroken. Alone. It wasn't worth it, no matter how handsome or funny or caring Nico was. He'd be gone, and she'd be left behind.

"Belllla!" exclaimed Madame, click-clacking through the reception area. "Your head is in the clouds today! Look lively, girl. Someone's coming."

Bella had been slouching on the desk, a mix of tired and dreamy, but now she sat up straight, fixing a smile on her face for…for…Valentina De'Medici.

Dressed in ankle-length skinny black pants, a black-and-white shell, and a tiny, trendy black blazer, with a Kate Spade purse and her blonde hair held back by Gucci sunglasses, she was the very picture of modern sophistication.

"Hello," said Bella, blinking in surprise at their unexpected guest. "Welcome, Miss De'Medici."

"De'Medici?" repeated Madame. "Not...*Valentina* De'Medici?"

"*Sì*," said Valentina with an arrogant shrug of her shoulders.

"Oh!" cried Madame, pressing a palm to her heart. "Oh, your Serene Highness! What an honor. May I congratulate you on your upcoming wedding? My goodness. How may we be of service?"

Bella's mouth dropped open as she stared at Valentina in shock.

Serene Highness?

A...princess?

Wait. A. Minute.

Her eyes widened in dismay as she recalled scoffing when Valentina asked for "hair for a princess." Was this true? And, Oh. My. God. If she was a princess, than her brother was a...a...

"Wouldn't that be something? To meet a real *Medici or Borghese?"*

"Think so?"

"The Italian nobility isn't nearly as famous as the British, of course. I mean, I could pick William or Harry out of a crowd, but plop an Italian prince in front of me and I'd have no idea."

She supposed that a black hole opening in the floor of the Innsbruck Salon and Spa and swallowing her whole was unlikely, but *Dio*, she'd never wished for anything more.

"*Thees* stylist girl," said Valentina, gesturing to Bella with a dismissive flick of her hand. "She *deed* my hair last night. Last minute. Now she comes to have lunch with me. *Subito*."

Madame's head jerked to face her goddaughter, her eyes wide. "Is this true? Were you of service to the De'Medicis last night, Bella?"

"Tina—that is, the princess, um, Princess Valentina—her royal...um..."

"*Serene Highness*," supplied Valentina, keeping a hand on her jutted hip and looking at neither Madame nor Bella, just posed as though the paparazzi would be arriving momentarily, and she'd be ready.

"She needed a last-minute updo!" finished Bella frantically. "And no one else was here."

"Yes. Yes," said Valentina, sighing. "We are *feenished* talking. She comes with me to have lunch. *Subito. Andiamo.*"

Bella looked at Madame, shrugging her shoulders and cringing as Madame fluttered her fingers around her throat. "B-But your Serene Highness, Bella has clients to—"

"I don't care about *thees*," said Valentina, looking at Madame like she was a flea on a junkyard dog. "She will be back later. *Ciao, signora.*"

"Yes. Yes, of course. Bella must join you for lunch. I am so sorry I questioned you." She turned to Bella with a wavering smile, whisking her hands at her goddaughter. "Bella? Why are you standing there? Her Serene Highness has invited you to lunch. *Andiamo! Subito!*"

Bella scurried from behind the desk, smoothing the sides of her intricate braid and tucking her crisp, white, button-down blouse into the waistband of her pink-and-white toile pencil skirt.

Following Valentina into the elevator, she turned to the princess—*princess!*—as soon as the doors closed.

"Princess Valentina, I had no idea who you were yesterday. You must allow me to apologize for—"

Valentina groaned and waved her away with another bored flick of her hand, then opened her purse, pulled out a card, and handed it to Bella.

On the front it read, in black script letters:

His Serene Highness Nicolo Alessandro Lorenzo Giovanni De'Medici

Her heart skipped a beat as she flipped it over to read:
The boathouse in Central Park 12:00·—Nico

"Your lunch *ees* with him, not me," she said, lowering her sunglasses, but damn if Bella didn't catch the slight tilt of her lips as she said it. "My brother talks about you all morning until I *keel* him or I go get you." She shrugged. "He *ees* my twin. I decide to let him *leeve*."

Bella's cheeks were aching from the width of her smile as she clutched the stiff white card in her hand. She chuckled softly. "*Grazie,* Valentina."

"*Prego*, Bella. *Ciao*," she said, striding out of the elevator and across the marble lobby without glancing back.

And Bella, who rarely left the New York Metro Tower Hotel at all, let alone for something as fun as a lunch date with a handsome prince, sailed through the lobby behind her, hailed a cab, and asked to be taken to the boathouse.

CHAPTER 3

"Are you angry?" asked Nico, grinning at her over a glass of Sauvignon Blanc.

He had greeted her with a customary, European two-cheek kiss, then held her chair for her as she sat down. Frankly, dressed in hip-hugging jeans and a pink button-down dress shirt rolled at the cuffs, he was even more beautiful than he'd been in a tuxedo last night. His eyes sparkled beneath sweeping, dark lashes, somehow mischievous and manly at the same time.

She cocked her head to the side, trying to look severe. "About you using your sister to lure me to lunch? Or because you failed to mention that you're an Italian prince?"

"Either?" he asked, cringing. "Both?"

"You might have mentioned that you were a prince when I was gushing about William and Harry," she pointed out.

"Fair enough," he said, shaking his head. "But you were so cute about it."

Cute? Huh. Was cute good? Was she cute like a kitten or a little sister? Or cute like a woman he'd like to kiss? she wondered, suddenly hoping for the latter, though she had no expectations. She was still trying to convince herself that she was actually playing hooky from work on a busy Saturday afternoon.

"Sorry, Bella." He shrugged. "My cousins get all the attention."

"Wait a minute," she said. "Do you actually *know* them?"

"Well," he said, trying desperately not to grin at her, "besides the fact that we're third cousins once removed, yes, we do run in some of the same circles."

Or used to...before the last of our fortune was mis-handled.

"The yachting, skiing, and polo circles?"

He chuckled, his good mood quickly restored by her sass. "More when we were younger than now. Everyone's so busy."

"Oh, yes. Buying castles and keeping up palaces is—"

"—villas," he corrected her with a grin.

"—so *exhausting*."

"Quite so," he said in a credible British accent, reaching for the bottle of wine. "Do you drink?"

"*Certo*." She nodded. "My parents owned *un piccolo vigneto*."

"A vineyard in Ticino?" He paused in his pouring. "Then surely you'd prefer a red?"

Perhaps it shouldn't have surprised her that he remembered she was from Ticino and knew the region was known primarily for its merlots, but it did. In the best possible curl-your-toes sort of way, it did, because it meant that he was keeping track of her.

"Not at all. I like white too," she said, "and Sauvignon Blanc is my favorite."

"Mine too," he said, pouring her a full glass. "My uncle's vineyard in Fiesole makes a mean bottle."

"*Dio!*" she exclaimed, pieces of information coming together in her head. "You're not talking about the *Villa De'Medici Vigneto!*"

"The very one," he said, raising his glass. "You know it?"

"I do," she answered, her mind segueing back to many happy afternoons spent touring the vineyards in and around Florence with her parents. "I remember it well."

"God, you're beautiful," he murmured, and she looked up at him, meeting his eyes, which had taken on a slightly pained look, like perhaps something was hurting him a little.

"Thank you, Ni—um, your Serene Highness?"

"No. Absolutely not. You are *not* calling me that. Nico, okay? Nico is who you met last night. Nico is who I am." He raised his glass. "And you're beautiful Bella, who keeps saving the day. *Salud.*"

Lifting her glass, she clinked his, shaking her head at his blatant flirtation. "*Salud.*"

He held her eyes as she took a sip of the chilled wine, savoring it on her tongue as her parents had taught her and breathing slowly through lightly parted lips to smell the bouquet before swallowing.

"It reminds me of *friulano*," she sighed, recalling a crisp, delicious regional white wine from northeastern Italy.

He grinned at her, swirling his glass absentmindedly. "Now *that's* my favorite wine of all."

"Mine too!"

"My uncle still makes one. He calls it *La Dolce Vita*."

"The sweet life," said Bella with a sigh, replacing her glass. "I've had it."

Nico leaned back in his chair, searching her face. "Tell me…did your boss give you a hard time about leaving with Tina?"

"I think she was so stunned to have a princess standing at her reception desk, she didn't have time to process what was happening. And your sister has a way of making her wishes…"

"…mandatory." He nodded. "Tina rarely *asks*. She much prefers to *order*."

"Well, it certainly worked with my *madrina*."

"Your *madr…*" He screwed up his face. "Your *godmother*? Your boss is your godmother?"

Bella nodded. "*Sí*. My parents died several years ago, and Madame Gothel brought me to New York. My parents were her childhood friends."

"I'm so sorry about your parents," said Nico, his eyes compassionate. "I'm not particularly close to mine, but still…if anything happened to them…"

"I miss them every day," said Bella, clearing her throat before taking another sip of wine. "But I am lucky to have Madame's help and guidance. She is training me in all facets of salon and spa management and ownership. I'm sure that someday the Innsbruck will be mine."

"Is she very old?" he asked.

"No. She's not fifty yet."

"It sounds like 'someday' is a long way off." His forehead creased. "Does she expect you to work this hard for the next twenty or thirty years? Cleaning and accounting and classes every night? Not being able to accept a date or have a little fun?"

"I *do* work hard, but…" Bella licked her lips. "I wasn't entirely truthful last night."

"How so?"

She leaned forward, lowering her voice. "It's true that I have to help her, but…well, I exaggerated my busyness last night. The truth is, I'm not allowed to date guests of the hotel. Not under any circumstances."

"Or what?" he asked, leaning forward and using the same conspiratorial voice as she.

"I don't..." She shrugged and shook her head, then grinned at him. "I don't know, actually. But I'm not seventeen anymore. She doesn't *have* to let me live with her. I guess she could...send me away."

"Back to Switzerland?"

"Ha!" scoffed Bella. "She's too frugal to put me on a plane back to Ticino. I guess I'd just be...out. You know—"

"On the streets?" he asked, his handsome face screwing up into a scowl.

She nodded, taking another sip of wine.

"Surely your parents left you something?" he asked.

She sighed. "All my money was given to Madame for my living expenses."

"And she didn't set any aside? So you could be independent one day?"

Bella thought about this for a moment. "I don't believe she wants me to be independent."

"Why would she?" asked Nico, scoffing with something that looked a little like disgust. "She'd lose her slave."

Cringing at the ugly word, Bella leaned away from him. "I'm *not* her slave."

"Really?" he asked, sitting back in his chair. "How much do you make for answering phones, fixing hair, staying after hours, cleaning, accounting—"

"You've made your point," she interrupted, feeling defensive.

"No, I really want to know," he said. "How much?"

She raised her chin, picking up her menu and scanning the words on the page, though she wasn't processing them at all. Without looking at him, she said in an even voice, "She brought me here when I had nowhere to go. I live rent-free in her apartment. I have my own bedroom and—and food. A credit card for incidentals. And I'm learning a trade. That doesn't ring of slavery to me."

"So you make nothing."

"I have free room, board, and an education."

"Chattel in velvet chains."

"What do you mean?" she asked, lowering her menu to meet his eyes with a frown.

"Property. A slave. A pet. Cared for in luxury, but far from free."

"A pet?" she cried.

"I mean no offense," he said quickly. "I just don't like the way you're being treated."

Well, she didn't like what he was saying about her, or about Madame, whom her parents had entrusted to raise Bella after their deaths. She looked down at the menu again. "It must be very easy to judge from your lofty position."

"No, Bella," he insisted. "My position isn't so very lofty. And actually, my life isn't so different from yours."

"Not different?" she asked. "You're a prince! Royalty! You can do whatever you—"

"—want to?" He shook his head. "No. I'm afraid not. Not at all." He cocked his head to the side. "Think about it—Tina doesn't want to marry Steve Trainor, does she? And yet…"

Bella thought about this. Valentina's circumstances—an impromptu wedding—certainly made a lot more sense now. She couldn't think of another European royal, aside from the Monaco royals, who'd ever had a child out of wedlock, and she imagined that titles and…and villas…wouldn't be passed down to those children, would they?

"No, she doesn't," said Bella, her heart filling with compassion for Nico and his sister. Maybe they were in similar circumstances, after all. What had he called it? *Chattel in velvet chains*…which made her wonder: "Who do *you* have to marry?"

***

Nico's heart sank a little as she asked this question, because even though he knew it wasn't right, he was hoping to sidestep it this week. He was hoping to spend the week—every waking moment—with Bella, but if he answered her honestly, there was every chance she'd refuse to see him again.

Still, looking into her clear brown eyes, he found he couldn't lie. He'd have to take his chances with the truth.

"Her name is Elena." He'd never seen anyone's eyes lose their sparkle so quickly, and it hurt him inside to see it. "Princess Elena of Greece and Denmark. Our families are old friends."

SHEAR *Heaven*

The smile she mustered was brave. "Friendship can be a good basis for marriage."

"To be clear, I haven't asked her yet...but I'm *supposed* to propose after Tina's wedding."

"Why *'supposed to'*?" she asked, her eyes compassionate as she reached for her wineglass and took a sip.

"The relationship between Italy and Greece is special," he said, reciting words he'd heard from infancy. "Our trade relations, especially. In fact, Greece is our most important economic partner. Our militaries collaborate. We share a lot of tourism. Strategically, they're one of our most important allies."

She nodded, urging him to continue.

"Plus, the De'Medicis...well, there isn't a delicate way to say this: we're broke," he said, "or quickly getting there. And Elena's family is very wealthy."

"Ahhh," she said, nodding as though figuring something out.

"What?"

"Last night...your sister mentioned her fiancé's fortune. I just—"

"—thought she was a money-grubber?" he asked sharply, ready to protect his sister, even if it was, partially, the truth.

"No," said Bella gently. "Please don't think that. I didn't judge her. I only noted that it was said."

"Sorry to snap at you," he said. "I hate that she has to marry a practical stranger for money and—and, a name for her baby."

"I understand. At least you'll be marrying a friend."

A friend? He barely knew Elena. Yes, they'd met each other at various functions throughout their childhoods, but he hadn't had an actual conversation with her in years. He had no idea if they were even compatible.

"There hasn't been"—he cleared his throat, feeling his cheeks flush with heat—"a marriage between the royal houses of Italy and Greece for some time. It would be a good thing."

"For whom?"

"Tourism? Trade? The world watching as an Italian prince marries a Greek princess?"

"But...will it be good for *you*?" she asked.

Frankly, he had no idea. But Valentina wouldn't get her settlement from Steve Trainor for ten years. His parents expected him to pay off their debts now with money from his future wife: Elena.

"As you say…marriages built on friendship are solid. Our families approve of the union."

A crease appeared on Bella's forehead as she folded her napkin and placed it on the table, looking up at him with heavy eyes. "I don't think it's appropriate for us to have lunch together."

Nico's hand darted out to reach for hers. "*Please* stay."

"You're almost engaged."

"But I'm not yet. Elena and I aren't even dating. We aren't together at all. Not yet." He rubbed slow circles in the soft skin of her palm. "Please. Don't go."

"It wouldn't hurt her, then? If she saw us together?"

Nico shook his head. "Not at all. I swear to you, we're not a couple. No promises have been made. My parents have spoken to hers, and her parents have welcomed the match if Elena agrees. But she's doing aid work in Africa. I doubt she knows anything about it yet."

She tried to pull her hand away. "Still…"

"Bella," he said, refusing to let go of her hand and deciding to put all his cards on the table, "since meeting you last night, you're all I can think about. And…I want to spend as much time as I can this week with you." He gulped. "While I'm still…free."

"Why?" she asked. "Why me?"

"Because you're beautiful and fun, and you don't treat me like a prince. Because you give great advice and make me laugh, and when I'm with you, the weight of the world slips from my shoulders. I promise not to kiss you, or fall in love with you, or try to make you mine…" He shrugged, then sighed. "I'm sorry. I guess I'm not a very good bargain."

"Let me decide that," she said, squeezing his hand before pulling hers away to place her napkin back on her lap. She looked up at him, her lips unable to keep her smile from spreading as she said softly, "I still have to work."

"Of course."

"So I don't know how much time we'll have."

"We'll make the most of what we do have."

"And no kissing," she said.

"Or falling in love," he promised, though he had a funny feeling in his heart that he wouldn't be able to keep it.

"We can be friends."

"Friends...," he murmured, knowing already that his feelings for her had surpassed friendship and hoping he could keep his end of the bargain.

"I wouldn't be able to forgive myself if I hurt someone...if I hurt Princess Elena."

"You won't hurt anyone, Bella...except me, if you refuse to see me again."

She grinned at him, shaking her head. "How am I supposed to say no to a prince?"

And for once, His Serene Highness Nicolo Alessandro Lorenzo Giovanni De'Medici was happy that he was a royal and didn't feel it a burden...because if that's what it took for Bella Capelli to spend time with him this week, he'd take it and say *Grazie*.

***

After lunch, he convinced her to let him take her for a rowboat ride, and she sat across from him in the sunshine, talking about her dismal lack of sight-seeing for the five years she'd lived in Manhattan.

"So," said Nico, his arms tanned and muscular as he rowed them farther out onto the little pond in the biggest city in the world, "you've never seen the Statue of Liberty, the ballet, the opera, the roof garden at the Met, a Yankees—"

"—or Mets!"

"—game, taken the Staten Island Ferry, or seen a Broadway show. Is that about the scope of it?" he asked.

Bella had stopped making excuses for her long days of work. "Yep. That's the gist of it."

"*Madonna*!" cried Nico. "That's unbelievable. You're in this great city, and you haven't seen a thing! Have you had a vacation in five years?"

Shaking her head back and forth, Bella said, "Nope. Not even a day off. I mean, unless you count Christmas...though I end up setting the table, making the dinner, and cleaning up after."

"Then I don't count Christmas," said Nico with a sour look. "When are you working tomorrow?"

"I have to be in at six a.m., but we close at three on Sundays, so I'll be finished by six!"

"A twelve-hour day?"

She nodded. "In early to get everything ready. Last to leave to make sure everything's in order. Remember…she's grooming me to take over."

"Will you be too tired to see me?"

Her bottom lip slipped between her teeth. *Never.* "No. It will give me something to look forward to all day."

"Me too." He nodded. "Okay. So out of all the things you've never done, which would you like to do first?"

The marquees of the many Broadway shows had taunted her on the few and rare occasions that she left the hotel. *What was it like*, she wondered, *to sit in a theater and watch people dance and sing who had the talent and courage to stand up in front of a full house?* She wished she could know.

"I see you thinking, Bella…What'll it be?"

"Have you already seen every show on Broadway?"

He chuckled at the way she backed into her answer with a question. "Not by a long shot. Shall we catch one together?"

She sighed longingly. "When I flew to New York, after my parents passed, there was a magazine in my seat back with an article about *Wicked.* You know, the play based on *The Wizard of Oz* characters? It all looked so wonderful."

"We'll go tomorrow," he promised, rowing them back toward the Loeb Boathouse.

"Can you afford it?" she asked, remembering their conversation at lunch.

"I'm a lawyer in Florence," he said. "I make a good living…just not enough to save the properties and businesses owned by the De'Medici family. If I only had to worry about myself…"

His heavy voice trailed off and they were silent as he rowed, the sound of the little boat cutting through the water and the ambient noise of other conversations drifting to her on the breeze. As much as Bella wanted to see a Broadway show sitting beside Prince Nico De'Medici, something inside of her felt unsettled.

Had she a right to spend these precious moments with a man who would soon belong to another? He had assured her that there were no promises between himself and Princess Elena, so technically, she wasn't doing anything wrong…but was she being smart?

Bella was the very definition of inexperienced. She had never really had a boyfriend, aside from a flirtation with another student from lower secondary school. But the extent of their love affair had consisted of a peck on the lips while walking home from a school play, which had made her innocent heart take flight. Was it wise, then, to agree to spend this time with Nico, who, she guessed, had had many love affairs and known many women? Looking up at him, at the way the sun kissed the gold strands in his brown hair, she knew that she was perilously close to falling for him already, and she barely knew him. What would happen, then, when he bid her good-bye and proposed to Princess Elena? How would she mend her broken heart?

I promise not to kiss you, or fall in love with you, or try to make you mine...

His promise returned to her, but she found little comfort in it. She was discovering, minute by minute, that it wasn't his love for her that would hurt her in the long run. No. It would be her love for him that could destroy her, that could leave a lasting and agonizing mark on her soul.

So don't fall in love with him, she told herself, chancing another glance at him through lowered lashes.

But how does a simple girl from a small town spend a week with a prince and say farewell with her wits and will intact?

She took a breath and sighed, looking ahead at the Bow Bridge just over Nico's shoulder.

"Tell me," he said gently.

"Tell you what?"

"Whatever's on your mind."

She slid her eyes from the bridge to his face. "I don't...I don't think it's a good idea to see you again."

He stopped rowing, his eyes narrowing in displeasure. "But Broadway...tomorrow...?"

She tried to smile, but couldn't.

"I'm sorry, Nico," she said, "but after a week of wonderful, I'll go back to my unwonderful life. And you..."

"I'll have to marry someone I don't love."

Bella gulped, her voice soft and uncertain as she stared at his throat, unable to look into his eyes. "If I spend any more time with you, I'll begin caring for you. I won't be able to help it."

"We could be friends," he said.

"No," she said, raising her gaze. "We couldn't."

"Please."

"I'm sorry," she whispered. "I think you'd better take me home."

***

Nico clenched his jaw as she dropped his eyes and turned away from him, feeling frustrated beyond belief. All he wanted was her company. All he wanted was to spend a little time with her. Was that so wrong?

Deep inside, he knew it was, because the moment he'd laid eyes on her last night, something had happened to his heart, and it didn't fall under the heading of "Friends." Not by a mile.

"I wish you'd reconsider," he bit out, his voice sounding rough and a little haughty.

"Please understand," she said as her bottom lip slipped between her teeth and held there for a moment. "I'm just trying to protect myself."

Huffing softly, he put some muscle into his erstwhile leisurely rowing, steering them back to the boathouse quickly.

"I'll walk you back to the hotel."

She nodded. "Thank you."

Nico stepped easily from the boat as a dockhand secured the bow line to a waiting cleat, then Nico offered his hand to Bella. She stared at it for a moment, her eyebrows furrowing, and he was just about to pull it away when she reached for it, clasping it to hers. Forcing himself not to smile or whoop with gladness, he pulled her up and onto the dock, then laced their fingers together, hoping she wouldn't pull away. And to his surprise and relief, she didn't.

The New York Metro Tower Hotel was about ten blocks south, so Nico set a strolling pace north toward the Shakespeare Garden, reluctant to hasten their farewell.

"I've already seen more today than I've seen in years," said Bella, and he had the feeling she was trying to lighten the mood between them. "I didn't know New York could feel so much like the country."

"Tell me what you miss the most about home," he said.

"My parents," she sighed. "But also the mountains and lakes. The air is so much fresher there. Have you been to Ticino?"

"Yes," he said. "A good friend of mine has a place on Lake Lugano."

"Mmm. That's the most popular spot of all. But you're missing out if you've never seen Lake Maggiore. Lesser known. Just as lovely."

"What else?" he asked, savoring the feel of her small hand nestled within his, her delicate fingers threaded through his.

She continued on about places she loved that he'd visited at some time or another, all of them fading in contrast to her loveliness, to the gentle cadence of her accented English. Did she have any idea how beautiful she was? How welcome she was in his lonely life?

Glancing to his left, where she walked beside him, he drank in the sight of her. She was dressed in a slim blue-and-white skirt and white blouse, with her long, thick hair braided and wound into a bun on the back of her neck. But some dark tendrils escaped, curling beside her ear, framing her face. He didn't miss the envious glances of the men who passed them, the lusty looks at her trim waist and small, rounded breasts, though Bella seemed oblivious to the attention.

As the only son of a royal family, there had always been high expectations on him. To make his family and Italy proud, to marry well, to have sons who would ensure the De'Medici line, to augment the family's dwindling fortune either by trade or by marriage…all of which would be handily met by marrying Princess Elena.

And yet, if he were just a regular man—a businessman in New York closing a deal or a tradesman attending a conference—how he would like to consider Bella more seriously. What he wouldn't give to be able to woo her…if that's what he wanted. Alas, it wasn't even something that he could consider if his position meant anything to him.

"…and I guess the wines too. Oh! And the polenta! It's better in Ticino than anywhere else in the world."

"Is anything *not* better in Ticino?" he asked, grinning down at her.

"Hmm. Well, we're technically part of Switzerland, of course, but sometimes…I mean, culturally speaking, we're very different. Culturally, we're Italian. The old men play *bocce,* and we eat *gelato,* and we're so much more relaxed than the rest of *Svizzera.* It's almost like a—a, um, a *crisi d'identità.*"

"An identity crisis."

"*Sí*," she confirmed. "An identity crisis. Am I Swiss? Yes. Am I Italian? Yes, again."

"Is it bad to be two things?" asked Nico, pulling her up the roughhewn steps into the garden, which was an explosion of color: red and blue tulips, pink magnolia blossoms, hot-pink and white impatiens, and yellow daffodils.

"Niiiiiico," she breathed, pausing at the top of the steps and squeezing his hand. "*Dio*. How beautiful!"

He turned to face her, watching her dark eyes widen with pleasure, her pink lips parting softly as she looked down the stone path that snaked through the verdant heaven in the middle of a thrumming city. And suddenly the sting of her rejection and her insistence that they not meet again, felt too terrible to bear. He turned to face her, pulling her into his arms, and parting his lips as he dropped them to meet hers.

She gasped in surprise and he let her breathe him in, moving his lips gently, tenderly, longingly over hers, his arm tightening around her as she whimpered softly and melted against him. Her breasts pressed against his shirt, and his body reacted instinctually to the soft pressure, tightening with want. Her hands, which had fallen loosely to her sides, now met behind his neck, lacing together to draw his face closer to hers.

He inhaled the scent of her—clean linen and fresh air and a slight taste of the wine they'd shared at lunch—and he knew that if heaven had a fragrance, he was smelling it now on earth. And he never wanted it to be farther than arm's reach from him again.

But Bella pulled away suddenly, unlocking her fingers with a gasp and staring up at Nico with a mixture of surprise and betrayal. Her chest heaved up and down with her shallow breathing, and she raised her hand to brush two fingers over her lips.

"Bella," he started, the look on her face making him reach for her, but she stepped back, out of his grasp.

"You promised. No kissing. No falling in love," she said softly, tears brightening her eyes. "And now...and now, you've gone and..."

"I'm not sorry," he said evenly, his only regret that the sweetest kiss he'd ever known would be the only one they'd ever share.

She gulped, looking down at her feet. "I have to go."

And just like that, he recanted. "Bella, I'm sorry. I promise…I won't touch you again. I won't—"

Her head snapped up, and she seized his eyes with hers. "But I *want* you to. Don't you see? That's the problem. Now that I know…Nico, I *want* you to touch me like that over and over again." She bit her lip, averting her eyes in misery. "Don't follow me."

She turned and started back down the stairs, and Nico felt panic grip him. Was this the end? Was their solitary day already over?

"Bella!" he cried. "Wait!"

She turned to look at him over her shoulder, reaching up to brush a tear from her cheek. "*Addio. Addio,* Nico."

Farewell.

She hurried down the rest of the steps, and Nico—who would ask Elena to be his wife at the end of the week—could do nothing but watch her go.

CHAPTER 4

"Well, I certainly hope she doesn't expect for you to entertain her *every* day!" complained Madame Gothel on Sunday afternoon. "We got so busy that *I* had to step in!"

God forbid you actually work *at the business you own.*

Careful that her *madrina* wouldn't see her eyes roll, Bella made certain her face was neutral before looking up. "I'm so sorry for the trouble, Madame."

"Oh, Bellllla, darling. It's not your fault. It's flattering, I suppose, that the princess would seek out your company," sniffed Madame. "Though I can't imagine whyyyyyy."

Bella looked up at her godmother, on her guard. "What do you mean?"

"Well, my dear," she said, holding out her hands palms up as she leaned her head to the side, "you're a simple country girl. Of what interest could you possibly beeeeeee to her?"

"We spoke about Ticino…about wine…about my parents—"

Madame Gothel sighed heavily, adding under her breath, "Stimulating conversation for a royal."

"She seemed to like me," murmured Bella, wondering if Nico had been faking his interest in her. Had she been boring to him? Provincial? Simple?

"Of course she did." Her godmother cupped her cheek. "You are a…pleasant sort of girl."

Bella stepped back, out of her godmother's reach.

"Madame," she started, then cleared her throat, mustering her courage. "I've been meaning to ask you. You are—I mean, you do *intend* to let me take over here someday, don't you?"

Madame Gothel's eyes widened, and she straightened her head, pursing her lips with displeasure as she stared at her goddaughter in surprise. "What a bold, inelegant question."

"I don't mean to offend you. I just assumed. The classes. The training. But we've never actually discussed it."

Her *madrina* chortled softly. "All that is so that you can be my *helper*, dearest."

Chattel in velvet chains.

"But my parents..." She was about to say, *But my parents always intended that I inherit and run the grotto and vineyard,* which is why she had assumed that Madame, who had no children, had planned to do the same with her business.

"Your parents...what?" Madame's expression grew instantly icy. "Were you about to refer to your parents' money? What *little* they gave me to care for you?"

"No," said Bella, though Nico's words returned to her: *Surely your parents left you something?* "But now that you mention it...did my parents leave me anything?"

"Yes." Madame raised her chin. "Pennies."

Bella thought back to her parents' business: to the wine bottles that they boxed and loaded onto a truck for distribution each year, to the seemingly endless crowds of tourists who kept the grotto busy all spring and summer long. Had they been in debt? Less successful than Bella remembered?

"Are you certain?" she dared to press.

"This is outrageous! You have lived under my roof, enjoying my hospitality, *dear* Bella, for five years now. Even if there had been anything when you arrived, it has certainly been spent by now."

"But, *Madrina*—"

"Enough!" shouted Madame Gothel, her eyes blazing. "One afternoon with a princess, and you return ungrateful and—and entitled. Well, I'll tell you what you're entitled to, pet: nothing. You're twenty-two years old now. When you're ready to move on, I certainly won't stand in your way."

Move on? thought Bella, a wave of panic making her chest tighten. *With what?* All she had was the cash tips that clients slipped into her hands without Madame's notice. It was barely enough for a week's stay at a seedy hotel, let alone enough to set up an independent life.

"No, Madame," she said, realizing how trapped she was. "I'm so grateful to you for—for everything. I didn't mean to sound entitled or ungrateful. You've been very good to me."

"That's right."

"Thank you, *Madrina*," she said softly.

"Well, now you've upset me," said her godmother, sniffing as she pulled her black cardigan sweater more snugly around her bony shoulders. "After *everything* I've done for you..." She whimpered softly, looking at Bella with eyes that were much more angry than hurt. "I think I'd better go and rest for the remainder of the afternoon. Close up at three. Clean up here. And be quiet when you come home. I need time to recover from this—this...*unpleasantness*."

"Yes, Madame," she said, watching her *madrina* turn and head for the glass doors.

At the last moment, Madame Gothel turned. "Out of respect for your mother, dear Karin, I took you in. But lest you have forgotten, you are *not*, in fact, my daughter or my blood. What I do for you, I do out of pity. Don't *ever* take me for granted again, Bella...or question my intentions."

"No, Madame," Bella whispered, tears biting at her eyes at the mention of her mother's name.

"Should it *ever* happen again, I fear we will need to say farewell, dearest," she said sharply. "Am I understood?"

"Yes," murmured Bella, lowering her head as her godmother entered the elevator and disappeared from view.

Oh, Mama. I miss you.

Bella took a deep, unsatisfying breath and shook her head.

There's no future here, she thought, reaching up to swipe at her eyes. *I'm trapped—just like Nico said. A slave. A...pet. Is this what you want, Bella? Is this the life you want? The future you want? If not, do something to change your fate.*

She thought about Nico—about his assertion that they were both trapped. But for the first time, she understood that she was not actually trapped in the same desperate way that he was. She could, in fact, if she planned carefully, choose to leave *this* life behind and create a *different* one. Nico, on the other hand, would be a prince from cradle to grave, with all the pressures and expectations of that birthright.

She sighed, sitting behind the reception desk as the unexpectedly quiet afternoon wore on, distracting herself by reviewing every precious detail of her date with Nico yesterday:

the surprise that he was a prince, the lovely lunch at the boathouse, the way he looked in the sunlight as he rowed her around the lake, the profusion of color in the gorgeous garden, and the way it felt to be kissed—*really* kissed—for the first time in her life.

Leaving him standing at the top of the stairs, his face remorseful, his voice desperate, had carved a hole in Bella's heart, and it ached now, throbbing as she traced the lines of his face in her mind. It hurt to know that he was here in the hotel for several more days but that she couldn't—or wouldn't—see him. She'd fallen hard for him yesterday, and subsequent dates would only make their final farewell unbearable.

Looking up, she found Greg, the Sunday concierge, exiting the elevator and opening the glass doors of the salon. Bella fixed a smile on her face, glancing down at the reservation book. No doubt Greg had some appointments to make.

"Hey, Bella," he said.

"Hi, Greg," she answered brightly. "Do you have some new clients for me?"

"Uh, no, actually." He placed an envelope on the shiny chrome surface between them. "This is for you."

"For me?"

Greg nodded. "For you. And I'm meant to say that if you require something to wear, you're to give your name at Maxime's and Renata will take care of you, all expenses paid."

"*Take care* of me?"

"Close the store. So you'll have privacy to shop."

Bella's mouth dropped open, and she stared at Greg, trying to understand what was going on. Maxime's was one of the hotel boutiques that sold top-of-the-line ladies fashions at exorbitant prices, and Renata was the store manager.

"I don't understand." She glanced down. "What's in the envelope?"

"I have no idea," said Greg. "It came to me via messenger with the express instruction that I personally deliver it to you, creating a distraction, if necessary, to be sure it was given to you in private."

"I…"

A small walkie-talkie on Greg's belt loop beeped twice, and he looked down at it. "Duty calls. See you around, Bella."

He turned and left the salon, pressing the elevator call

button and stepping into the lift as soon as it arrived. Picking up the envelope, Bella stared at it for a moment before opening it.

The first thing she withdrew was a ticket to the eight o'clock performance of *Wicked*. Gasping with surprise, she giggled softly with delight as she stared at it pinched between her fingers, noting the seat was *ORCH D-102*. She knew enough about Broadway theaters to know that the ticket she held in her hands was for a seat somewhere in the front/middle of the theater—a *perfect* and very expensive seat.

The second thing she withdrew was a note. It had no signature, nor a greeting. It read simply, *Please*.

Nico.

Her heart soared as she held the ticket in one hand and the note in the other.

Whatever willpower she'd mustered yesterday disappeared like a puff of smoke, and she sighed with happiness. She would choose wonderful with him, and suffer unwonderful without him later.

How in the world could she say no?

***

Nico had arrived at the theater thirty minutes in advance and had been seated promptly. But now, with five minutes left before the show was supposed to start, his hopes were waning. Bella had been quite firm with him yesterday about being unable—or unwilling—to see him again, and truly he understood why. She was right to avoid him. Smart. He was, as he'd observed to her yesterday, a bad bet—a man spoken for, for all intents and purposes. And yet he couldn't give up on the sheer pleasure of her company without one last try. It was probably playing dirty to offer her a ticket to the one show she wanted so desperately to see, but offering her any less than her heart's desire seemed pointless. As for arranging a private session at Maxime's? He didn't want to give her an excuse to say no. While his allowance was meager compared with other princes of Europe, it was certainly enough to spoil a pretty girl a little.

And yet it appeared that his careful plans were in vain. Turning back toward the stage, he sighed in disappointment. With three minutes until curtain, it looked like he'd be watching the play alone.

More's the better, he tried to convince himself. *Why should she and I get to know each other better, creating wonderful memories, when we have to say good-bye on Friday? What's the point?* He rubbed the beard on his chin, trying to make peace with his situation. *She's wise to stay away.*

"*Mi scusi, credo che questo è il mio posto.*" *Pardon me, but I think that's my seat.*

His heart started racing as a smile burst across his face. Nico looked up to see a goddess standing beside him, grinning down at him with her wonderfully warm, fresh, familiar smile. He leaped to his feet, drinking in the sight of her face as she tilted her head back to look up at him.

"Bella," he murmured. "*Tu sei qui. Sei belissima!*" *You're here. And you're so beautiful.*

"*Grazie*," she said, dipping into a small curtsy before looking back up at him. "I couldn't resist."

"Nor could I," he said, trying to hear her over the fierce hammering of his heart.

Her lips were pink and glossy, and her long, dark tresses were curled and pinned back, falling over her shoulders and halfway down her back. Pale pink and gauzy, the knee-length dress she wore fit her petite frame perfectly, making her look even more angelic and innocent than usual. His eyes trailed over her body covetously, his mouth watering as he traced the lines of her bare legs.

"You're a vision."

"I'm returning the dress tomorrow," she said, easing past him to take her seat, her small breasts brushing against the crisp, white cotton of his dress shirt.

"The hell you are," he muttered. "I'll tell them not to accept it."

"Don't make me regret coming," she said, sitting gracefully in the maroon velvet seat before looking up at him with no-nonsense brown eyes.

"Fine. Return it," he muttered, taking his seat beside her as the lights went down.

But when the orchestra started playing the overture, he reached for her hand, taking it in his gently, weaving their fingers together and desperately hoping she wouldn't pull away.

What would it be like, he wondered, to marry for love instead of duty? To come home to someone like Bella every night? No doubt she would run around the vineyard rows with their children, laughing and warm, and at night—*O, Dio*—at night, he would hold her small body in his arms, the softness of her breasts falling over his forearm, her curves fitting perfectly against him, skin to skin, reaching for each other under the covers before finally sleeping.

A brief vision of Princess Elena flashed through his head—his mother had e-mailed Nico a picture of her this afternoon. She was accompanying a UN Peacekeeping mission through Ethiopia right now, and the picture was of her—with her short blonde hair, angular body, dust-covered face and serious expression—holding a starving black child in her arms.

Elena was a good person. *Such* a good person.

He would try his best to do right by her. To be good enough for her. To make his family proud.

But for now…just for now, in his last, precious moments of freedom, he would selfishly forget about her and concentrate on the lovely girl beside him. Turning just slightly, Nico watched Bella's face in profile: her wide eyes and parted lips, her swanlike neck long and graceful in the half light from the stage. He'd tasted those lips, and it had only whetted his appetite further.

He heard an echo of laughter in his head, felt a quick flash of longing as he thought of Bella chasing their children through a sunlit vineyard…

No, insisted his brain, shutting down the heavenly vision.

It would never be.

Though he was falling for her madly, there was no future for them, and dreaming of it would only make saying good-bye harder.

***

"*O, Dio*!" she cried softly, turning to face him as the lights came up. "Isn't it wonderful?"

"You're enjoying it?" he asked, grinning at her exuberance.

She sighed. "The way she flew! The special effects are just…" She grinned at him, cocking her head to the side. "Am I going on and on?"

"Am I complaining?"

"No," she said, but she felt self-conscious, recalling

Madame's harsh words, ...*you're a simple country girl.* "But I don't want to bore you."

"*Bore* me?" he asked, his eyebrows furrowing. "You're the most fascinating person I've ever met."

"Ha. A simple country girl from Ticino? Right."

"I mean it, Bella," he insisted. "You're just…you. All your emotions on the surface. All your words honest and true. No games. No angles."

"Angles?"

"When you're a prince, sometimes it feels like everyone's working an angle."

"Hmm," she said, her heart clenching, "I'm sorry for that. It must be a terrible way to live your life."

His expression lightened. "Tonight, nothing is terrible. Tonight, *cara* Bella, everything is perfect because you're here beside me."

"Prince Charming," she teased.

He leaned forward and pressed his lips to hers—the sweetest, lightest touch, but Bella felt it in her toes.

"For you? Yes. I will be as charming as possible." He stood up, still holding her hand. "And to that end, *cara*, how about a glass of champagne?"

"I'd love it," said Bella, letting him lead her up the aisle.

After their bubbly, they resumed their seats for the second act, which was even more emotional than the first, and Bella found herself crying by the end, a surprise reunion between two characters making her heart full to bursting.

A handkerchief appeared in her hand, and she wiped her cheeks gently, careful not to smear her carefully applied makeup. She'd enjoyed dressing up like a princess just for tonight—doing her hair, makeup, and nails in the quiet salon after everyone had gone home, then visiting Renata to choose a dress. Renata had tried to convince her to choose a sexy black cocktail dress, but it didn't feel at all like Bella. When she saw the pale-pink tulle, goddess-style cocktail dress, she hadn't been able to look away. And from the look on Nico's face when she arrived, it had been the right choice.

As he led her from the theater after the show, they found horses and carriages for hire outside, and Nico insisted that they take a ride together. The evening had grown chilly during their show, so the driver handed them a nubby wool blanket that Nico laid across their laps before putting his arm around her shoulders and pulling her snugly against him.

Though the sensible part of Bella's brain knew that she should insist on finding a cab and heading home alone, she couldn't resist the romance of a moonlight carriage ride with a prince. She sighed in happiness, laying her head on his shoulder and closing her eyes as they clip-clopped away from Times Square and toward Central Park.

"Why'd you come?" asked Nico softly, his deep voice close to her ear.

"I couldn't stay away," she answered honestly.

"I shouldn't have invited you," he said, holding her closer, his hand heavy and warm on her upper arm, where he rubbed gently.

"I shouldn't have said yes."

"But you did."

"I did," she said, opening her eyes and tilting her head back to look up at him. "And I would again."

"Would you? If I asked you to meet me tomorrow? You would?"

She nodded. "There's no use resisting you. As long as you're here...I won't say no again."

Her words sounded forlorn, though, and Nico flinched.

"Bella," he said, "I don't want to hurt you. I can—I mean, I *will* leave you alone...if you tell me to. I'll tell the driver to stop. I'll say good-night and leave this carriage. I'll pay him to take you home, and I won't bother you again. I promise."

"That would hurt me more," she said, her eyes dropping briefly to his lips before skating back up to meet his gaze.

"We only have a handful of days...and even those are spoken for. The rehearsal and dinner on Friday. The wedding on Saturday. Elena will be here by then and..."

She reached up and placed a finger over his lips, her eyes fluttering at the soft warmth of his skin. "Then we have until Friday. And it's only Sunday."

"Five days." His lips puckered as he kissed her finger softly. "I promised I wouldn't kiss you before. But I can't promise that now."

"I didn't ask you to."

"So we'll...see each other? For the next few days and then...?"

"Say farewell," she said, refusing to let her eyes brighten with tears. "I heard this in a movie once: *I'd rather have thirty minutes of wonderful than a lifetime of nothing special.* That's how I feel about you. About us."

"Ah, Bella. *Cara, bellisima* Bella. Me too," he said, bending his head so that his lips found hers.

His hand cupped her jaw, a gentle pressure that kept her lips exactly where he wanted them. She felt the gentle swipe of his tongue alone the seam of their lips, and she parted them, welcoming him into her mouth. As he slid his tongue against hers, a warmth, a heat, pooled in her stomach, then lower, making her shift against him, arching her back so that her breasts pressed against his chest. He groaned softly, holding her tighter, his tongue swirling around hers as his lips changed angles so that they fit more perfectly together. She threaded her hands into his hair, reveling in the thick softness against her fingers as she memorized the taste and texture of him.

And for Bella, who'd known very little love in her life, this felt like love.

It wasn't, of course.

It would be impossible to fall in love with someone so quickly—even a handsome prince who seemed determined to treat her like his princess for this one fleeting week.

But it *felt* like love, and Bella didn't fight that feeling.

"Tomorrow, Bella," he said urgently, his breath kissing her skin as his lips skimmed the column of her throat. "When can I see you tomorrow?"

Her fingers were still tangled in his hair, but now she loosened them, trying to think a clear thought. "Tomorrow is…"

"Monday," he said, his throat rumbling with a low, sexy chuckle.

"Monday. Right." She leaned back, looking up into his eyes. "The salon is closed, but it *is* a deep-cleaning day, and I'm expected to be there."

"Could you fake sick?"

She shook her head. "No. That wouldn't get me out of working."

His expression darkened. "You're not allowed to be sick?"

She shrugged, knowing he wouldn't like the answer.

"What about Tina? I could send her up to steal you again."

"Would she do it?"

"She's my twin sister. She'd do anything for me."

Bella grinned at him, nodding her head in relief. "Madame won't be able to say no. Valentina is very…persuasive."

"What time shall I send her?"

"Around noon? I'll help in the morning. It'll make Madame more amenable."

"And what do you want to do tomorrow, *cara* Bella?" he asked, nuzzling her nose, brushing her lips lightly with his.

"I don't care," she answered honestly, reaching up to cup his bristly cheek, "as long as I'm with you."

His eyes darkened, and his expression became serious. "How will I leave you on Friday?"

"Don't think about it," said Bella, pulling his face down to hers, her lips hungry for another kiss before the carriage arrived back at the hotel.

"But I'm greedy," he murmured. "I won't want to give you up."

"Let's not ask for eternity," she said softly, "when we have now."

Then she stopped any further conversation by pressing her lips against his, sinking into the warmth of his embrace as the summer stars smiled down on them.

CHAPTER 5

With her hair twisted back into a heavy bun at the base of her neck, Bella used her wrist to push some flyaway strands from her forehead. She wore heavy rubber gloves on her hands because using this much bleach to scrub floors and sinks once a week left her skin chapped and sore.

But every so often she'd take a peek at the clock on the wall. It was now eleven fifty, and with three of the four sinks thoroughly scrubbed, she only had one more to go. She doused the white porcelain in bleach, letting it saturate the sides for a moment before she'd start scrubbing.

"Belllla!" called Madame Gothel. "Almost finished with those sinks?"

"One more to go!" she answered, sighing as she picked up her scrub brush.

Madame had been fast asleep, snoring away, when Bella returned home last night, which was a relief. She may have been able to explain the dress by saying she'd bought it on Amazon with her credit card, but when the statement came at the end of June, Madame would know she was lying. Besides, she would have read it on Bella's face, wouldn't she? That dreamy, starstruck expression that Bella herself could hardly keep contained?

She wanted to make the very most of her five days, but that would only be possible if Madame didn't find out that Bella was dating a hotel guest. After their conversation yesterday, Bella knew now, in no uncertain terms, that Madame would have no problem turning Bella out of her home.

"Bella," said Madame, entering the hair-wash room

wearing a fashionable dress, her hair coifed and nails perfect, "hurry up, please. We still have the stations to do. And the reception area. You're pokey today, dearest. All you've managed to do is the bathroom, steam room and treatment room."

"Yes, *Madrina*," she said, sighing softly as she rinsed out the bleach, leaving the hair-wash basin sparkling clean.

Madame Gothel cleared her throat, and Bella looked up expectantly as she grabbed a towel to dry the sinks.

"Bella, I was certain I heard you come in late last night. Almost midnight, I believe."

Bella gulped, trying her best not to look guilty. "I was—I was on the roof for a while, Madame."

"Hmmm," hummed Madame Gothel, narrowing her eyes just slightly. "I see." She cocked her head to the side, a brittle smile on her face. "Alone?"

"Quite alone," said Bella.

"Alone on the roof wearing a…" She drew out her question, examining Bella's face, which felt hot under Madame's scrutiny. "…Chiara Boni limited edition?"

Bella took a breath, turning back to the sink and drying the remaining droplets rigorously. "I—I saw it at Maxime's—"

"So did I," said Madame, "so imagine my surprise when I also saw it hanging on the back of your closet door while you were showering this morning."

"I just wanted…to try it."

"Did you buy it with *my* card?"

"No, *Madrina!* I mean, I'm returning it today. I just wanted—I just wanted to try it on."

She finished drying the four sinks, then turned to face her godmother, knowing that her cheeks were probably red and hoping that Madame Gothel attributed this color to Bella's hard work, not her lies.

Madame gave Bella a long, hard look before shrugging elegantly. "Let me give you some advice, Bella, darling: don't indulge expensive taste. You haven't the means for it. Understand?"

With a relief she tried to conceal, she nodded. "Yes, *Madrina*."

"Return it promptly."

"Of course."

"And don't be so reckless again. That dress costs five hundred dollars. If you were to have soiled it—"

"I'm sorry!" Bella bit out.

Madame Gothel had turned to leave, but she stopped and pivoted, her eyebrows high with surprise as she looked back at Bella. "You don't sound very sorry, Bella. You sound almost…indignant."

"No, Madame," she said through clenched teeth, staring at the floor, making her voice more penitent. "I *am* sorry."

"All the same," said Madame, "why don't you give me your credit card for the rest of the week?"

Bella straightened, her lips parting in surprise. If Madame took the card away, all Bella would have was her meager tips.

"Please," she said. "You don't need to take my card away."

"*Your* card?"

"I'm—I'm very sorry," she said, her voice genuinely contrite. "I promise I won't do anything so thoughtless again."

"Of course you won't. Because not having an allowance this week will remind you to be more careful," said Madame with a cold, brittle grin.

Reaching into her pocket for the change purse that held a few dollars and her solitary credit card, Bella withdrew it and handed it to her godmother.

"It's for your own good, my dear," said Madame, pocketing the card. "I'm teaching you how to be more responsible." She brightened up, backing away from Bella. "I'm not all heartless. Take a quick break for lunch before you finish the rest of your work."

The lump in Bella's throat was so big she could do little more than nod miserably as her godmother left her in peace.

This is rock bottom, she thought, her eyes swimming with tears. *No money. No freedom. No love.* Fighting back her tears as best she could, Bella took off the rubber gloves, her heart heavy as she walked from the hair-wash stations toward the front of the salon.

"Your Serene Hiiiiighness! We are closed today! I am soooooo—"

"Stop talking," barked an annoyed voice in heavily accented English.

Bella paused in her steps when she heard her godmother welcome Valentina. Reaching up, she swiped at her eyes, an unexpected chuckle making her shoulders shake when Valentina essentially told Madame to shut up.

"Go get *zee* girl. Bella. I am so bored. I need her."

"Oh, your—your grace," sighed Madame, "I am terribly soooooorry, but she is not here."

"What do you talk about? Where *ees* she?"

"B-Bella? Oh, well. She is…um, s-sick today. Yes. *So* sick. Not at all well. A cough. Bless her sweet, simple heart. Her health is very delica—"

"She *ees* not here?" demanded Valentina. "You are for certain?"

"N-No. She is not here," said Madame, her voice slightly less certain as she continued lying. "Perhaps the hotel concierge could arrange an amusement for you? I could call down—"

The part of her that was still good, dutiful Bella, a pet in velvet chains, honestly considered staying silent around the corner, because she knew that was what was expected of her. But since meeting Nico, her eyes had been opened to the degrading, eroding awfulness of her life, and though she had no alternate plan devised yet, she certainly wasn't going to let Madame keep her from what small happiness she had.

"Madame?" she chirped, walking purposely into the reception area. "The sinks are finishe—oh, Princess Valentina. *Buongiorno*."

Valentina took one look at her, then slid her withering, unblinking gaze to Madame Gothel. "You say she *ees*…sick?" She turned to Bella. *"Sei malato?"* Are you sick?

"*No, non sto male, non ho mai sentito meglio,*" she said, pressing her palm to her T-shirt as though surprised by the question. *I don't feel bad. Not at all.*

Valentina's dark, hawkish eyes skated back to Madame, her lip turning up in a sneer as she stepped toward the older woman, fury written across her aristocratic features. "You lie to me?"

"Signorina, per favore—" Miss, please—

"Principessa!" shrieked Valentina, stomping he foot.

"Sì! Sì! S-Sua Alta S-Serenitá!" sputtered Madame. *Your Serene Highness!* "I—I am so—!"

"Stop talking," said Valentina, waving her hand dismissively at Madame Gothel. "You are…*liar*. Don't speak." She turned to Bella. *"Pranzo con me?"* Have lunch with me?

"I would love to," said Bella, flicking a glance at her boss. "But I have to work."

"Bella is...my helper, your highness, and I don't know if I can spare—"

Valentina's eyes blazed as she advanced on Madame, issuing a scathing tirade in Italian: *"Sei pazzo? Chi sei tu? Un bugiardo! Dirò ai miei amici di non venire—"* *Are you crazy? Who are you? A liar! I'm going to tell all my friends not to come to this—*

"Va bene! Va bene! Per piacere, principessa!" exclaimed Madame Gothel, raising her hands palms up in supplication. "She can go. She can go. Of course. I will find someone else to...to clean..." Madame turned to Bella, her expression a mixture of frustrated and furious. "Go, Bella! Why are you standing there?"

"Whatever you say, *Madrina*," said Bella, offering her guardian a syrupy-sweet smile as she followed Valentina into the elevator.

As the chrome doors closed, Valentina pressed the button for the nineteenth floor and wrinkled her nose. "You smell like a...washerwoman."

"I was cleaning."

"You can borrow my clothes to meet Nico," she said, staring straight ahead. "Your godmother is...*una strega.*" *...a witch.*

"*Sí*," agreed Bella, though it hurt her a little to admit it.

For several years, Madame Gothel had been Bella's only mother figure. Only now, when she could see Madame's true colors, did she realize that there wasn't a maternal bone in her godmother's body. She was selfish and self-centered, a shameless user.

The elevator doors opened, and Valentina led the way down the hallway, swiping her keycard at the door reader and preceding Bella into the suite. She turned to face Bella once the door had closed.

"He cares for you," she said.

Bella gulped. "I care for him."

"You know—you know he plans to marry *la Principessa Elena*?"

"Yes."

"It *ees* a mistake," said Valentina, placing her hand over her flat stomach. "*I* have no choice. He does."

Bella's eyes flicked to Valentina's hand. "You *are* marrying for love...even if it doesn't feel like it."

She nodded. "Steven Trainor *ees* not a bad man. He *ees* a *gay* man. So we will marry for a while, then we will divorce. But my child will be...*como se dice*...ah! *Legittimo.* Carina or Giuseppe Trainor. *Ees* not so bad."

"Can you be happy?" asked Bella.

"For now? *Sí. Il romanza rosa* will come later in life for me," said Valentina pragmatically. "Come now. *Andiamo.*"

Bella nodded, following Valentina into her bedroom. The princess opened the closet doors and withdrew a stunning white-lace sundress, handing it to Bella. "Maybe a *leettle* big. Nico won't care."

"Thank you," said Bella, turning her back to the princess as she took off her soiled T-shirt and jeans.

"Understand, Bella: Nico *ees* my brother, my twin, and twins, we have a special bond, yes?"

Bella nodded. "From what I understand."

"He doesn't love Elena. He *won't* love her. He has no—*como se dice*—uh, *passion* for *thees* girl. But he has passion for you."

"Will you zip me?" asked Bella, briefly making eye contact with Valentina over her shoulder. "Nico is doing what he thinks is right for your family."

Valentina zipped up the dress, placed her hands on Bella's shoulders, and turned her around so the women were facing each other. "But *eet ees* wrong for his heart."

Feeling helpless, Bella looked up into eyes so similar to Nico's, it made her heart pinch. But what could she do? She'd only known the prince for a handful of days. She wasn't his girlfriend. She was barely his friend. And yet...she felt things *with* Nico, and *for* Nico, that she'd never felt before in her life. And the thought of him marrying Princess Elena was like a knife through her heart.

Suddenly Valentina brightened. "You look okay now." She withdrew a card from the back pocket of her dark skinny jeans and handed it to Bella. "He *ees* waiting for you, Bella. *Andiamo.*"

***

Nico had received a text from his sister five minutes ago saying that Bella was in a taxi on her way to meet him. And if he'd had any doubt about what the girl from Ticino was starting to mean to him, it was abundantly clear by the way his heart took flight reading Tina's words.

Standing on West Street, at the corner of Vesey, he couldn't wait to introduce Bella to her next New York adventure: lunch at One, on the 101st floor of the Freedom Tower at One World Observatory. Not only was the view one of the best in New York, but they'd have a peek at the Statue of Liberty and Ellis Island before boarding a ferry at 3:00 p.m. to visit the gateway to America in person. He couldn't think of a more appropriate way for two visitors on U.S. soil to spend the day, and besides, as Bella's self-appointed Manhattan tour guide, it was his duty to be sure she saw as many of the sights as he could fit in by Friday.

Friday, he thought with a sigh.

His mother, who was back at home in Italy packing for her trip to New York, had called him today. Nico's father had spoken to Elena's father, Prince Phillip of Greece and Denmark, on the phone this morning, reconfirming his permission for Nico to propose to Elena.

"Nico!" said his mother, Her Serene Highness Caterina De'Medici, breathless with excitement, "We're all so excited!"

"*Vero?*" he'd muttered. *Is that right?*

"*Sì!*" his mother had crowed. "Elena is coming straight to New York from Ethiopia, where she's…she's…well, honestly, darling, I have no idea what she's doing there, but she's coming directly to Manhattan from Africa, so Phillip won't have much time to discuss the proposal with her in advance. Perhaps that's for the best. You have what you need, Nico: his permission to ask her."

He'd sighed, trying to picture himself approaching the perennially-tanned, tall, muscular princess and asking her if she was interested in a royal union. There was no sense in trying to make it romantic. It wasn't. It was—for all intents and purposes—an arranged marriage between two royal families.

He was silent for so long, his mother spoke again, her voice softer this time: "She's a good person, Elena. Very kind. Very rich."

Not-so-subtle reminders that he should make the best of

things, since the De'Medici clan could certainly use an infusion of wealth.

"I know, Mother," he said. "I always liked Elena."

"Love can grow from like," said his mother. "And with time."

But can passion? wondered Nico, already knowing the answer in his heart.

Yes, love—true affection—could grow with time, of course, But attraction—and passion, for that matter—wasn't a quality that could reliably develop. You were either attracted to someone, or you weren't. And if you weren't, no amount of trying could force your heart to lift when you saw someone. And if you were, no amount of trying could persuade your heart *not* to lift when you did.

"Mother, I've so much to do," he said, feeling uncomfortable discussing the matter any further. "You'll forgive me?"

"Of course, darling! See you on Friday! And keep Tina in line, *por Dio*! We've almost saved her from disaster!"

And you, mother, and your greediness.

"Safe travels."

"*Ciao*, Nico."

"*Ciao, mia madre.*"

Now, as he scanned the street for unlit cabs, he felt—yet again—the same discomfort he'd felt talking to his mother. Was it possible he was making a mistake? Was it possible that by dutifully marrying well for the sake of his family, that he'd be giving up his chance for passion? For true love? For true happiness?

He frowned at the notion.

Last week, before he'd set eyes on Bella, it was something that hadn't really occurred to him. He'd been carefully conditioned his entire life to put family and duty first, above all else. But now? Having met someone special who lit a fire of longing within him, it was impossible not to wonder.

A cab pulled up to the curb, and he glimpsed her smiling face through the open back window even before the cab stopped. As he opened the door and handed the driver twenty dollars, all thoughts about Elena were whisked away as the object of his most fervent passion was suddenly in his arms again.

***

"*Buongiorno,* Bella," he said, his voice husky, his arms around her strong and familiar.

"*Ciao,* Nico," she said, closing her eyes and inhaling the wonderful smell of Acqua Nobile and warm cotton.

He drew away from her just long enough to place a finger under her chin and tip her head back. She smiled up at him but kept her eyes closed as his soft lips landed on hers, coaxing them apart. He kissed her gently, holding her tightly in his arms, and she wound hers around his neck, brushing the bristles on the back of his neck with her fingers and sighing with pleasure.

"I won't be able to stop if I kiss you anymore," he sighed by her ear. "Plus, we're in public."

She finally opened her eyes, squinting as she looked up at him. "Then what do you suggest?"

He cocked his head to the side and shrugged in a gesture that was so macho Italian, she almost giggled.

"What I *want* and what's *allowed* are two different things, *cara.*"

"Do we have rules about what's allowed?" she asked as he released her, exchanging an embrace for hand-holding as he pulled her into the building.

"We should," he said.

"Why?"

"Because I can't make you any promises."

"I haven't asked for any," she said, stepping on the escalator in front of him.

"Okay…because I'm a gentleman. And you're…*sei ingenuo.*" *Naïve.*

Hmm. She asked over her shoulder, "How do you know that?"

He leaned closer, because she felt his breath on her throat as he whispered, "I just know, *mi tesoro.*"

My darling.

Her breath caught and her heart squeezed with the soft, sensual sound of his lips near her ear. As the escalator ended, she was so distracted, she would have slipped were it not for his hand under her elbow.

"Careful, *cara,*" he said, laughter plain in his voice.

"Maybe *you* should be careful," she advised tartly, pulling her arm away. "I may not be as innocent as you think."

"Believe me, *cara mia*," he said, grinning at her, "there are moments I *wish* that was the case." His eyes, soft and tender, scanned hers. "But it's not, is it?"

She pursed her lips, refusing to answer, because really and truly, what grown woman wants to be outed as a virgin when she's on a hot date with a handsome prince?

Her silence answered his questions, and Nico chuckled softly beside her as he gave their tickets to an attendant, and they boarded what appeared to be a glass elevator. But as the doors closed and they started rising, she realized that the elevator was covered with movie screens that were showing the development of Manhattan Island from the 1500s to today. She watched as Indian dwellings magically turned into colonial buildings, and then streets appeared and suddenly skyscrapers. There's a bridge being built! There's the Statue of Liberty! And soon—way too soon!—the doors opened at the 102nd-floor observatory.

Her stomach was full of butterflies.

"Wasn't that amazing?"

He nodded. "It was! I've never seen anything like it!"

She looked ahead at the windows, showcasing a clear, dramatic 360-degree view of Manhattan before and beneath them. "Nico! Look!"

She dragged him over to the windows, and they stood side by side, admiring the view of the Hudson River and New York Harbor.

"We're on top of the world," she breathed.

"Do you remember what happened here in 2001?" he asked, his eyes tracking an airplane in the distance.

She gulped. "Of course. I was only seven years old, but I remember my mother crying for the people killed here."

He nodded. "My parents had friends who died."

"It was a terrible thing," she said, leaning back against him, "for the whole world."

From behind her, he wrapped his arms around her waist, resting his chin on her shoulder, and they stood like that for a few minutes, looking at the glorious view, quiet but for their breathing, which quickly synchronized—*in and out, in and out*—in long, comfortable draws of air.

"Are you hungry?" he asked her.

"Always," she said, turning slightly to grin at him.

He kissed her quickly. "Then let's go have lunch! Our cruise leaves in ninety minutes."

They spoke of Italy and Switzerland over lunch, gleefully swapping stories of their favorite childhood memories, and all the while Bella felt herself falling for him—deeper and more certainly every second. He was self-deprecating and smart, gallant and unbelievably gorgeous, and though she knew she was spoiling things for herself by anticipating their farewell, she couldn't totally ignore the fact that today was Monday, which meant that they only had four days left together. There was no getting out of work tomorrow. Madame had made it clear time and again—if Bella dated a hotel guest, she would be thrown out. She couldn't afford to raise Madame's suspicions.

As he stood behind her on the windy boat deck, with tendrils of her hair surely whipping him in the nose, what was he thinking? Was he beginning to feel desperate, as she was, for more time?

But that wasn't the deal, was it?

They'd agreed: a week.

A week and no more.

***

Nico sensed a sadness in Bella as they toured the Statue of Liberty, then got back on the boat for their transfer to Ellis Island. She'd become more subdued as the day wore on, and perhaps he was imagining it, but it seemed like her smiles were more forced, her sighs deeper.

"Is everything okay?" he finally asked, taking her hand as they disembarked, stepping onto a sidewalk that led to the Ellis Island visitor center.

"I'm afraid you were right about me," she said. Her hair was back in a long braid, but flyaway hairs had escaped around her face, and she pushed one behind her ear. "I *am* naïve."

"I was only teasing," he said. "I love that about you—how fresh and honest you are. I didn't mean to make you feel bad."

"I thought I could do this," she continued. "Be your— your…I don't know—your sort-of *ragazza* for a week," she said, using the word for *girlfriend*. "But now I wonder…"

His chest tightened. "What? What do you wonder?"

She sighed. "Remember last night? When I said that we shouldn't get greedy for more when we have now?"

"Mm-hm."

"You're not the only one feeling greedy now," she confessed.

"Want to stop?" he asked, holding his breath.

"You mean...stop seeing you?" she asked.

"Yeah. We can, uh..." He gestured to the boat. "We can get back on the boat. I'll take you home. We can..."

She shook her head, entwining her fingers through his and squeezing. "No. We can't."

"I don't want you to be sad."

"But sad's part of it," she said, facing him and tenderly cupping his cheek, "isn't it? Falling for someone isn't safe. It's...exhilarating and wonderful. And yes, I'd rather have it than not. But you must allow me these moments of sadness. Of knowing that what I have now is so perfect yet so finite."

"I wish there was another way, but it seems..." He clenched his jaw. "My parents have already spoken to Elena's parents. They have offered the union. It's as good as done."

"I see," said Bella softly, blinking her eyes quickly before looking down at their shoes.

A bolt of something miserable slammed through his chest as he watched her bow her head, and suddenly he couldn't put her through this anymore.

"I'm taking you back to the hotel," he said. "I'm a selfish bastard for letting this go as far as it—"

But she was up on tiptoes, her lips pressing insistently against his as her breasts brushed his chest. And he was helpless to resist her, pulling her into his arms, against his body, with a crushing embrace, hating himself and loving her. *Loving* her. Wait. *Loving* her? No. *No, that's not right*, his brain insisted before a fog of lust replaced rational thought, the soft slide of her tongue against his chasing all logical ideas out of his head. He could feel the thrumming of her heart through the white sundress she wore, feel her shudder with need, bowing her back toward him in natural, unpracticed sensuality, her body wanting more of his, even though he was quite certain she'd never made love before.

I want to be your first, he thought suddenly. *I want to be the first man to have you.*

His body reacted instantly, his cock stiffening between them, pressing against her belly as he held her tight.

It wasn't right, but he couldn't help it. He'd never wanted anyone the way he wanted her.

"A-hem," grumbled a voice from behind them, and Bella jerked her head back. "Don't mind kids necking, but *you two* may want to get a room."

Nico looked over his shoulder at a white-haired park attendant. "Sorry."

"No harm done. Why don't you go look at the museum, huh? Only have an hour until closing."

Nico nodded, looking down at Bella's face. At her bee-stung lips and heavy eyes. She was so lovely, so trusting. No matter what, he promised, he wouldn't take her innocence. Not if he couldn't offer her anything more than a sweet summer fling.

"Shall I take you back?"

"No," she said, mustering a smile and lifting her chin. "I want as much time with you as I can have."

"Me too," he said, sighing in relief.

"But I might get sad," she said, shrugging.

"Me too," he said again, tucking a tendril of long black hair behind her ear. "Can I see you tomorrow?"

She nodded. "But no sending Valentina. Madame's going to be on the warpath after today. I can meet you at eight. *After* work."

It frustrated him that they'd lose a whole day, but he couldn't jeopardize her relationship with her godmother. "Fine. Meet me on the roof?"

She nodded, her face transformed by a huge smile. "My favorite place."

"You're *my* favorite place, Bella Capelli." He leaned down and kissed her gently. "Now, no more, uh, necking. We've got a museum to see."

CHAPTER 6

Every quiet minute on Tuesday felt like an hour as Bella kept glancing at the clock, waiting, waiting, waiting for the day to end.

Luckily, most of the day was actually very busy.

At ten o'clock, she saw ancient New York socialite Mrs. Madeline Winters, who needed a wash, blow-dry, and roller set in her white hair.

At one o'clock, frequent hotel guest and pop singer Samara Silvestry required a touch-up on her ombré with Joaquin, followed by a wash and braided updo with Bella.

And at four thirty, twin sisters and heiresses Veronica and Victoria Van Dussel came in for identical updos, which took a good bit of time, because the twelve-year-olds insisted that no one be able to tell them apart, which essentially meant that not a wisp of hair could be out of place.

By six o'clock, Bella was tired, sitting at the reception desk, answering messages, and booking appointments, but as the staff bid their good-byes at seven, her heart, and mood, lifted. Madame Gothel had shot Bella several dirty looks but otherwise avoided her for most of the day.

"Bella, I need to speak with you," said Madame, stopping by the reception desk, her face pinched. "We simply cannot allow what happened yesterday to happen again."

"Madame?"

"The Princess Valentina has no respect for your position here, and I fear you encourage her behavior. I'm afraid if you accept her invitation again and skip out of work like it doesn't matter to you, I will have no choice but to fire you."

"*Fire* me?"

"From your position here."

She kept an indignant scoff to herself. "But I don't even make a salary, Madame."

"Your room and board is your salary, Bella."

Bella stared at her godmother in shock. "You mean that if the princess asks me to lunch again and I go with her, you will force me out on the street?"

"That's an awfully dire way to look at it."

"How else *can* I look at it?"

"As a way to politely assert yourself, dearest," she said, grinning at Bella, though the gesture didn't crinkle her eyes with any affection. "As an opportunity to refuse the princess while still preserving the relationship."

"But, Madame, *you* are the one who told me to go."

"Yes. But next time, I won't be here. If I see her coming, I will excuse myself and let you manage it."

"And I'm meant to say *no* to her?"

"You are. Politely, of course, so she isn't offended."

"You've met her!" insisted Bella. "She's not the type of woman you say no to."

Madame steeled her shoulders and lifted her chin. "Nor am I."

Bella gulped, finally understanding that had she continued on as Madame's grateful workhorse indefinitely, things may have stayed amicable between them. But by questioning her godmother and winning Valentina's favor, she had upset the apple cart, and things would never go back to the way they were.

"I'm so glad we chatted," said Madame. "I'm going to have a nice, long bath. Clean up in here, and be quiet when you come home just in case I'm already asleep." She turned away and headed for the glass doors.

"Why did you take me in?" Bella asked her back. "You don't want me here. I'm not sure you ever did."

Madame turned to look at Bella, cocking her head to the side as she stared at her young ward. "Your mother...Karin...looked more German than Italian. Blonde. Blue-eyed. But your father..." She paused, a hint of real emotion tracking across her face, her eyes briefly shuttering in pain before opening again. "Giorgio was dark like you. Jet-black hair. Olive skin. Eyes that could reach into your very..." Her voice faded away, and she snapped her lips shut, clenching her jaw.

Finally, she said, "To be frank, I had no idea you'd look so much like *him*."

Bella was almost trembling, trying to follow all the spoken—and unspoken—things Madame was saying. "Why—why does it matter that I look like my father?"

Madame's eyes narrowed. "It doesn't. Stop asking me these stupid questions."

Jerking around, she pushed through the glass doors and didn't turn to look at Bella again as she waited for the elevator to arrive.

It took Bella a full minute to move from where she stood frozen behind the reception desk.

What in the world did it mean? Had Madame Gothel—Helga—had feelings for her father? Bella searched her mind, but she could never remember her godmother visiting them in Bellinzona. Though she did recall a framed photo on the little piano—three young teenagers, arm in arm: beautiful, blonde Karin, who smiled at the camera; tall, handsome, dark-haired Giorgio in the middle, who stared at Karin; and plainer Helga, who faced forward but didn't smile at all.

Had Helga been in love with Giorgio? And had he been so firmly in love with Karin that he hadn't noticed? Had her mother known?

Bella thought back to the picture of the three teenagers.

No, she decided. Her mother hadn't known of Helga's feelings. Neither, she guessed, had her father.

When Bella arrived in the United States, had Helga Gothel hoped against hope that Bella would resemble her mother, Karin? Blonde and blue-eyed? Instead, she'd stepped off the plane, the spitting image and same age as the teenaged boy in the picture. A boy who had broken her heart.

Bella felt a wave of sadness for Madame Gothel, who'd married a man for money in her thirties and likely never known true, requited love. Did it hurt every time she looked at Bella? Did it ache to remember the way Giorgio looked at Karin?

Walking in a daze to the supply closet, Bella took out the Windex and spritzed the counter, wiping it distractedly.

"*L'amore è un campo di battaglia,*" she said softly as she rolled up her sleeves to tidy the rest of the salon before racing up to the roof to see her forbidden prince.

Love is a battlefield.

***

Nico had thought of everything: a soft blanket, votive candles, a basket full of gourmet Italian treats that the hotel concierge had tracked down in Little Italy, plus plates, napkins, utensils, wineglasses, and a bottle of Ticino Merlot that hadn't been easy to find. He'd thought about asking the concierge to rope white lights around the roof but recalled Bella's warning that they weren't actually permitted up there, so he made do with the moon, stars, and candlelight, which cast a warm glow onto the blanket. It was a stunning sight—their cozy picnic with the lights of Manhattan beyond.

But it all paled in comparison to her.

It was the look on Bella's face when she came around the corner and found him that he would always remember.

She was wearing the same denim skirt she'd been wearing last Friday night when he'd first met her, this time with a white T-shirt that accentuated her small, round breasts and tiny waist. Her hair, held back with a simple black hairband, fell down her back, tumbling in glorious waves past her hips. And on her feet she wore tiny black shoes that looked a little like ballet slippers.

As she ran to him, her eyes sparkling with happiness, he opened his arms wide for her, catching her against his chest and urgently finding her lips with his. He wound his arms around her slight body, holding her close, feeling the panting breaths that forced her breasts against his chest. She moaned into his mouth, and he swallowed the intoxicating sound, committing it to memory so that once he was married and his bride was far from home in Africa, he could recall the sweet murmurs of the lovely girl he'd met in Manhattan.

"*Merda*," he cursed softly, leaning away from her, knowing that such a memory shouldn't be captured and held for such purposes. He hadn't even proposed to Elena yet, and he was already planning ways to cheat on her with his mind and his heart.

"What?" asked Bella, her smile glorious in her upturned face.

"Nothing, *cara*," he said, smiling back at her. "You. Just you. You make me lose my mind."

She arched her back, teasing him a little by rubbing against him. "Today was so long."

"For me too."

"What did you do?" she asked.

"Thought of you. Planned a picnic. Thought of you some more."

She looked around his arm at the *piccolo festa* he'd laid out on the blanket and gasped. "Is that a *Rosso della Piana* Merlot?"

He nodded, smiling at her delight. "It is."

"I know the *Vitivinicola San Mateo*," she exclaimed, pushing out of his arms to kneel down on the blanket and reach lovingly for the open, breathing bottle. "It's in Cagiallo!"

Shoving his hands in his pockets, he stared down at her, his heart throbbing with affection for her.

"They have a lovely little tasting room," she continued. "And...and a white dog. Named Flo."

"Flo?"

Her grin didn't waver as she looked up at him and nodded. "*Sì*. My parents knew the owners. Before they..."

"Died," he said gently.

"Yes," she said, cocking her head to the side. "You know, I think I figured something out tonight."

He kicked off his flip-flops and lowered his body to the blanket as she poured two glasses of wine for them. Lying on his side, he looked up at her. "What?"

"I think my *madrina* was in love with my father."

Nico's brow furrowed. "You mean he cheated on your mother?"

Bella looked up from her work. "No! Never!"

"Then...?"

"They were childhood friends, but two girls and one boy...you can imagine how much it must have hurt her that he loved my mother. She came here when she was eighteen, just after my father proposed. I think—I mean, I wonder if she left, partially, because it was hard to see her best friend marry the man she loved." She handed Nico a glass of wine. "Here. Try it."

Nico swirled the wine around the glass before taking a small sip. It was rich and full-bodied, but not too overbearing. "It's good."

"It's a Carminoir grape," said Bella after taking a sip. She sighed with pleasure. "Thank you for this."

"For you, *cara* Bella? Anything." He reached for a

piece of cured meat, popping it between his lips. "So you think your *madrina* was in love with your father?"

"Yes," she said thoughtfully. "I think that's why she treats me so badly...because I remind her of him—of the man who didn't love her back."

Nico swallowed the *salumi* and reached for a small wedge of cheese. "It doesn't make her behavior okay."

"But it does explain it," said Bella, placing her wineglass on the paved roof, then repositioning herself so she was lying on her back, looking up at the stars. "And there's comfort in understanding. I didn't do anything wrong. It isn't me. It's her...or him, I guess."

Nico shifted a little closer to her, staring at her profile. "Did you *think* it was you?"

She turned her neck to catch his eyes. "Of course."

He took another sip of wine, then placed his glass on top of the closed basket, leaning closer to her. "You thought you did something wrong?"

"I thought, perhaps, that I wasn't very likeable."

"Bella," he breathed, unable to bear her words. He lay on his back beside her, staring into her eyes. "You are an angel. You are sweet and kind, gentle and honest. How could you ever think you were unlikeable?"

With a small smile on her lovely face, she stared at him for what felt like a long, long time before whispering, "Nico."

"*Cosa, mia cara?*" *What, my love?*

"*Baciami,*" she murmured. *Kiss me.*

He held his breath as his eyes flicked to her sweet pink lips. Reaching out to rest his hand on her hip and pull her to him, his nose nuzzled hers gently, and he heard her gasp. Just a swift intake of breath that stole the last of his self-control. His lips sought and captured hers as she reached up to cup his jaw. He nipped at her lips, testing the softness of the top between his, and then the bottom, inhaling the mix of fragrances that was Bella after a day around shampoos and sprays. She was still on her back, and Nico changed position slightly, slanting his body over hers, his chest resting lightly on hers, his elbows bracketing her head.

She pulled his head down to hers, and he swept his tongue into her mouth, groaning softly as she curled her fingernails into his scalp and exhaled a sexy whimper. Spreading her legs with his knee, he nestled between them, still kissing her, sliding his palm under her T-shirt, beneath her bra, to cover the soft fullness of her breast.

As she dragged in a ragged breath, he skimmed his lips to her throat, rubbing her nipple with his thumb as he licked and kissed the soft skin of her neck. She tilted her head back, and he glanced up at her face—eyes closed, pillowed lips parted—and all the blood in his body raced to his cock, which hardened to steel. He thrust lightly against her as his lips slid to her chest. As he pulled his hand from her breast, he pushed her bra and T-shirt to the side and took the hard bud of her nipple between his lips.

Arching her back, Bella moaned softly as he sucked on her flesh, her breath shallow and ragged as he slid his lips across her chest and bared her other breast to his kiss. Rolling one nipple gently between his fingers, he laved the other with his tongue, listening to the sounds of her moans and whimpers, reveling in the instinctual way her hips rose to meet his again and again in a rocking rhythm of their own making.

"Bella," he whispered, blowing softly on the slick nub of distended flesh.

"Hmmm?" she murmured.

"I care about you," he said, using the bare remnants of his self-control to cover her beautiful breasts with her bra, then smoothing her T-shirt back over the satiny cups. "I've never wanted a woman as badly as I want you. But…" He braced himself over her, looking down at her, staring into her eyes. "You mean something to me. Something real."

"Nico," she murmured, her voice thick with need as she slid her hands from his hair to his cheeks and pulled his lips down to hers. She kissed him passionately, fiercely, their teeth clashing and tongues dancing as he let his weight fall against her, plunging his hands into her mane of hair and holding on.

He pushed against her, his throbbing cock sliding into the valley of her legs through his pants and her skirt, hard as stone and aching for more. More that he couldn't have. More that he *shouldn't* have.

He leaned away from her, panting, staring down at her in agony, part of him wishing that he was the kind of man who would take what he wanted and deal with the consequences later. But he wasn't that man. And Bella, far less experienced than most of the women he'd been with, wasn't a woman to be used and left behind.

Heaving himself to the side, he rolled off of her onto his back, staring up at the pinkish-blue sky, lit up by the millions of city lights below. His chest rose swiftly up and down as his lungs inflated and compressed, and he ran a hand over his brow, sighing because of the things he wanted, because of the things he wouldn't let himself have.

Twisting his neck, he looked over at her to find her tongue wetting her lips, one arm thrown over her eyes. Ribbons of heat, of yearning, emanated from her body like electricity. He felt them. He recognized them because they unfurled from his too.

"We can't," he said softly.

"I want it so badly too," she murmured, as though she could feel his eyes on her.

"But I would be your first," he said, leaning up on his side to face her.

"Yes."

"And then we would say good-bye."

She clenched her jaw and swallowed. "Yes."

"I can't do that to you, *cara*."

She moved her arm, looking up at him with sparkling eyes. She wasn't crying, which made him feel relieved, but there was such sadness in her expression that it wasn't much comfort.

"My *madrina*...how she must have suffered wanting what she couldn't have. Watching her best friend fall in love and get engaged. Knowing that the boy she loved—the *man* she loved—would never love her the way she wanted him to."

"It hardened her," said Nico, sitting up and grabbing his wineglass. "I don't want the same for you."

Bella folded her hands on her stomach, just under her breasts, still staring up at the sky.

"We don't have to...make love," she said finally, looking over at him with a hopeful expression. A slight, shy smile curled her lips, and her dark eyes twinkled. "But that still leaves a lot, doesn't it?"

He smiled at her because he couldn't help it. "It does."

"So lie down beside me, handsome prince," she sighed, "and kiss me some more."

***

They had stayed on the roof together until almost midnight,

making out, finishing the bottle of wine, and sampling the Italian treats. Nico had kissed and caressed her breasts again, and Bella had delighted in the wicked feeling of her sensitive skin bared to the cool night air. She had felt that part of him—that manly part of him that she'd never seen or touched before—grinding against her, and it had made her feel weak and wanton, desperate for things that would break her heart later.

She had agreed to see him again tonight—she had an accounting class at City College from six until eight, but Nico said he'd pick her up after class and take her out to dinner.

As she leaned her cheek against her palm, sitting at the reception desk, she tried to muster some gratitude for the way he'd stopped them from going any further, but it was hard, so very hard, to feel grateful when she wanted so much more than she could have.

Looking up, she saw Greg step off the elevator and through the glass doors at the same time Madame Gothel swept into the reception area.

"For meeeeee, Gregory?" she asked, gesturing to the bouquet of red roses he held in his arms.

"Uh, no, ma'am. For Bella, actually."

Madame's eyes shot to Bella, who wiped the bursting smile off her face and tried to look shocked instead. "What?"

"For, uh…for Bella. They were dropped off at the reception desk by the Princess Valentina."

"Oh," said Bella, flicking a glance at her godmother, whose eyebrows were bunched together in confusion and anger.

"The princess sent flowers for *Bella*?"

"She dropped them off with me. Yes, ma'am." Greg nodded at each of them, depositing the enormous bouquet on the reception desk and then turning and heading back toward the elevator.

Madame Gothel's eyes lingered on the roses for a long moment before she raised her glare to Bella. "Why is the princess sending you roses, Bella?"

"I have no idea. Perhaps there's a card that explains?"

Madam took the bouquet of flowers before Bella could collect them and inspected them for a card. "No. None."

Bella gulped nervously. "Maybe they're to thank me for having lunch with her?"

With narrowed eyes, Madame slowly placed the

flowers back on the counter. "I am not a fool, Bella Capelli. Play me for one, and you will lose."

"I'm not playing games," she said.

"I heard you come in at midnight last night. Were you with the princess?" Madame leaned closer to Bella. "The rumor around the hotel is that the princess's wedding to the Trainor billionaire is a sham. Perhaps she's not interested in him. Or men at all, for that matter. Perhaps she's interested…in you."

Bella couldn't help it: she chortled at the thought of Valentina hitting on her. "I *highly* doubt it."

"Just remember, Bella, dating *any* hotel guest, of *any* sex, would break our agreement. Yes?"

"Yes, ma'am," said Bella.

"A hotel employee who dates the guests is little better than a prostitute," she reminded Bella in hushed tones. "And sluts who fuck guests certainly don't live under *my* roof."

Bella's cheeks flared with heat as she stared back at Madame.

"Understood," she whispered.

"Wonderful," said Madame Gothel, backing away from the reception desk and turning back into the salon.

I have to get out of here.
I have to get out of here.
As soon as Nico is gone, I will figure out a plan.

***

"So tell me," said Nico, offering her his arm as he picked her up after class, "how was Excel for the Masses?"

"Dull," said Bella with a sigh. "Madame insisted that I take the class, and honestly? I like being here at college once a week. But the class itself? Ugh."

"She wanted you to learn Excel for work?"

Bella nodded. "I split my time between styling hair, answering phones, and helping her with the books."

"And cooking and cleaning."

"And cooking and cleaning," she agreed with a heavy sigh.

"Tell me this…what would you study if you could choose any subject?" he asked.

"Hmm." She paused. "I'd be a sommelier, maybe. Or a chef."

"So you'd go to culinary school."

"Yes! Definitely!" she exclaimed, holding his arm tighter as he led them over to Fifth Avenue, then turned left to head downtown. "You went to college."

"Of course," he said. "And law school."

"You're far better educated than I am. I only have a secondary-school diploma."

"You can go back and get a degree whenever you're ready."

"It's very expensive here," she said.

"But not at home," he reminded her. "There are many public universities in Switzerland."

"That's true," she said, nodding her head as though it hadn't occurred to her before. "I guess I don't think of myself as Swiss anymore...Well, I mean, I do! Of course I do. It's my home...where I grew up. Italian is my first language, but I'm fluent in German and French, of course, too."

"And English."

"*Everyone* in Switzerland speaks English," she said, rolling her eyes at him. "I guess I just mean that I don't think of myself as a *Swiss-living* person anymore."

"Because your life is here."

She stopped walking and faced him. "My *life*? What kind of life is this? Chattel in velvet chains to a woman who can't stand the sight of me. She hates me, and I...well, I don't like her very much either." She giggled suddenly, as though shocked by the confession. "Whatever my mother once loved about her friend Helga is long gone now. I don't like her one bit!"

Nico chuckled with her, then leaned forward to cup her face and kiss her tenderly.

"Then change your fate," he whispered against her lips, stopping in front of a little bistro where they had a reservation for dinner, and desperately wishing he could do the same. Before he turned melancholy, he looked down, into her beautiful brown eyes. "Meet me up on the roof after dinner?"

She nodded. "Of course."

"And tomorrow night too, Bella? It's...our last night together?"

He saw the hesitation flare in her eyes, the moment of concern for herself and maybe even a little bit for him. Because the feelings between them were real, and saying good-bye or forgetting each other seemed almost as impossible as an Italian prince changing his destiny for a hair stylist from Switzerland.

But she was brave, his Bella.
She lifted her little chin and nodded.

CHAPTER 7

After dinner last night, Nico and Bella had held hands, strolling down Fifth Avenue like they had all the time in the world, when really it was winding down like crazy. They entered the hotel lobby separately, but ten minutes later, they met on the roof, falling into each other's arms and kissing for hours. At one point, Bella had even fallen asleep on Nico's chest, her ear over his heart and her body snuggled against his.

And that's when she'd known—in those warm, dark moments of disappearing time before her eyes had fluttered closed—that she was in love with him.

And it didn't matter that she'd known him for less than a week.

Or that she was a country girl and he was an Italian prince.

Or that he was older and infinitely more sophisticated than she.

It didn't matter that she had no money and he had to marry for it.

Or that she had no solid and safe plan for her life.

Or that she lived in New York and he'd be leaving for Florence on Sunday.

None of it mattered.

None of it could have shaken the certainty of her feelings.

This was the feeling that had shone in her father's eyes when he looked at her mother; this was the dream deep and safe in the furthest reaches of every woman's beating heart. This feeling. The absoluteness of it.

She held on to it, even made a lullaby of it, letting the words *Ti amo* slip between every beat of his heart as she drifted off to sleep.

He'd shaken her awake an hour later when the hands of every clock they could see on the skyline pointed straight to heaven. It was already midnight, and besides the fact that she needed to be at work by six tomorrow, if she wasn't careful, she'd find the locks changed on the penthouse door one evening soon.

They'd kissed good-bye, and Bella had known a sudden courage as she assured him that she'd find him on the roof for their final night tomorrow. No more tears. No more grieving for what could never be. Just a quiet certainty that there was nothing left to save herself from; love had come, and there was no sense anticipating the fracturing of her heart now because it was a foregone conclusion. She knew, with a new sense of enlightenment, that she may have found the love of her life in Nico De'Medici, to whom she'd already given her heart. And yes, it might be a long life of yearning if she never saw him again, but her wish for thirty minutes of wonderful over a lifetime of nothing special had come true.

So when she climbed up the stairs on Thursday evening after work, it was with the intention of holding nothing back and having no regrets. If she was to live the rest of her life without her heart, the least she could do was honor her feelings by not being sad or afraid. There would be plenty of time for sadness and fear. Tonight? Tonight was all about love.

"You're here," he said the moment she opened the door and walked into the stairwell.

"You scared me!" she said, placing her palm over her chest and giggling, breathless with happiness to see him again.

He reached for her, cupping the back of her head and kissing her in the dark cement hallway before leaning away. "I would have waited in the corridor, but I didn't want anyone to see me. This was the closest I could get to the elevator. Come on. I'm all set up."

Taking her hand, he climbed the stairs to the roof, pulling her behind him.

Like last night, he'd organized a little picnic for them, complete with another bottle of Ticino Merlot and his iPhone playing soft music.

"I thought I'd take a risk with the music," he said. "Do you like Christina Perri?"

She nodded. "I loved the *Twilight* movies. Her song "A Thousand Years" was sort of their theme."

As "Sea of Lovers" started playing, he raised his hands to her. "Dance with me?"

He shucked off his flip-flops, and she toed off her ballet flats, stepping into his arms. She placed one hand on his shoulder and pressed her other palm against his. He wrapped one arm around her waist and pulled her closer, looking deeply into her eyes.

> *Sea of lovers losing time*
> *And lovers losing hope*
> *Will you let me follow you*
> *Wherever you go*

"Oh, Bella," he breathed, his voice gravelly with aching longing, breaking with emotion.

He pulled her flush against him as the thrumming drumbeat kicked in, his arms locking around her waist and his fingers curling into her lower back. His breath was shallow, short bursts of misery against the skin of her neck as they moved slowly together.

"Don't be sad," she whispered, looping her arms around his neck to press her heart closer to his, and resting her cheek against his shoulder as they rocked to the music.

> *Will you let me follow you*
> *Wherever you go*
> *Bring me home*

As Christina Perri's voice faded away, Bella breathed deeply.

"I'm going home," she said softly.

"Right now?" he asked, his voice clipped with panic.

"No," she said, leaning back to look up at him. "I mean...I'm going back to Ticino, Nico."

His eyes scanned hers. "When?"

"As soon as I can manage it." She sighed, smiling up at him. "This isn't my home. Not really. And after today..." She tilted her head to the side. "I will always remember our days in New York, but I think I'd rather think of it as a fairytale. A perfect, imaginary time. A big, beautiful city where handsome princes fall in love with—" She gasped. "*Oh, Dio*! I didn't mean you'd fallen..."

"It's true," he said, nodding slowly, holding her eyes with a searing intensity. "It's the truth. Say it. Say what you were going to say. I want to hear you say it."

"Okay." She nodded at him. "...a big, beautiful city where handsome princes fall in love with country girls from little towns far, far away."

He clenched his jaw, still nodding at her. "I did. I fell in love with you."

"So did I," she admitted, chuckling bitterly. "Stupid us."

"Stupid us."

"I'm not sorry," she said. "I'm not sorry that I found you. I'm not sorry I fell in love with you."

"Me neither," he said, his eyes darkening as they flicked to her lips, then trailed slowly back up her face. "I'll never forget you, Bella."

"Nico...," she said, determined to tell him what she wanted before she lost her nerve. "Remember on Tuesday night? When you said that you wouldn't be my first? That you wouldn't do that to me?"

"I remember."

"I *want* you to be my first."

"Bella—"

"I'm not a child. I'm a grown woman and I'm making this decision for myself. I want you to be my first. I want...you. All of you."

***

The part of him that wanted to protect her, to keep her from making a mistake that she might regret for the rest of her life, was overruled by the simple and miraculous fact that they loved each other. He didn't care that he was all but promised to someone else; tonight he was still free, and tonight his heart, and his body, would belong to no one but Bella.

She took his hand and led him over to the blanket, reaching down for the hem of her dress and pulling it over her head.

Without touching her or dropping his eyes to look at her body, he reached behind his neck and pulled his T-shirt and dress shirt over his head, standing bare-chested before her. Reaching for his belt buckle, he unfastened it, then unbuttoned and unzipped his jeans, wiggling a little so they fell to his ankles. Kicking them away, he took a step toward her

Standing almost naked in the moonlight, she reached behind her neck and pulled several pins from her hair, letting it tumble over her shoulders. Then she unclasped her bra and let it slip down her arms and to the rooftop with a whisper.

Suddenly her face exploded into a smile, and she let her eyes fall, sliding tenderly down his throat, over the ridges of muscle on his chest, and lingering at the bulge in his underwear before dropping them to his feet.

Following her example and thirsty to drink in her beauty, he savored the curve of her neck and the delicate arc of her small shoulders. Her breasts—small, rounded orbs of sensitive flesh—made his heart race. He dropped his eyes to her smooth, flat belly, then to the black panties that covered the part of her he craved so desperately. Her legs, surprisingly long and pale, were slightly knock-kneed, which made his chest swell with so much love he wondered how he could possibly bear it all.

Staring at her tiny feet, he realized, yet again, how much bigger he was than she, and not willing to frighten her, he held out his hand, keeping his eyes down until he felt her fingers lace between his. When he looked up, she was staring at his erection.

"Will it hurt?" she asked, sliding her eyes up to meet his.

"We'll go slow."

She nodded, her chest rising and falling as she took a deep breath. "I trust you."

"Just for tonight," he said, sweeping her into his arms before dropping to his knees on the blanket and laying her gently against the softness, "you're mine, *cara*. And just for tonight, I'm yours."

Leaning over her, he reached for the black lace of her panties, pulling them over her slim hips and down her legs, baring her to the night and to him—to his eyes, to his lips, to his mouth, which watered for a taste of her.

Kneeling between her legs, he leaned down, letting his bare chest press gently against hers as he kissed her deeply, his tongue slipping between her lips to find hers. He flattened his forearms on either side of her head and loved her mouth with his, rubbing her breasts with his chest, thrusting lightly against her naked body as he kissed her.

Sliding his lips down the graceful column of her throat, he inhaled her smell, nuzzling her warm, soft skin, wishing that he had a thousand nights like this one instead of just one. How he would have worshipped the night, gratitude bursting in his heart for the honor of loving her under the moon, under the stars, in their bed, under the covers, forever.

Her fingers tangled in his hair as he sucked one of her pert nipples between his lips, running his tongue slowly over the ridges of her hardened flesh, letting his teeth raze her skin gently, which elicited a moan from her lips.

He chuckled against her skin, circling her other nipple with the tip of his tongue as Christina Perri sang passionately about the thousand years that he and this particular Bella would never have together.

Covering her breasts with his palms to keep them warm, he kissed a trail down her soft belly, wondering what it would have looked like swollen with his children, their hands and feet wiggling beneath her skin, her laughter as she pressed his palm against her flesh, asking if he could feel it too. Banishing the beautiful dream from his mind, he slid his hands down her sides, over the slight swell of her hips, as he glanced up at her face. Slack with passion, her lips were parted, her eyes closed, her neck arched back—the most naturally sensual woman he'd ever known in his life.

"Bella," he said, letting his palm skate to the hint of soft hair covering her pussy. "I care about you so much."

"I know," she sighed, her voice thick and heavy. "Please, Nico."

He doubted she even knew what exactly she was asking for, but he couldn't wait any longer to taste her sweetness. Spreading her soft, delicate lips, he dipped his head and touched his tongue to the slick nub of hidden flesh.

Bella whimpered, her hips bucking from the blanket, and Nico slid his hands under her hips, cradling her in his arms as his tongue licked and sucked, circling her sensitive clit before drawing away to blow softly on the throbbing flesh. She was wet and writhing, ready for him.

Leaning back on his knees, he pulled his boxer briefs over his pulsing erection, then stood quickly and pushed them over his hips, letting them fall to his ankles and stepping out of them.

Beneath him, Bella looked up and smiled. "Look at you."

"I was just thinking the same thing."

"The moon's right over your shoulder," she said. "It's like you're standing in the middle of it,"

Katy Regnery

"The man in the moon," he said, smiling down at her.

"*My* man in the moon," she corrected him.

He knelt down between her legs, leaning forward to kiss her again. "Are you sure you want this?"

She reached for his face, cupping his cheek. "I'm sure."

He bit his lip. "I don't have protection, Bella."

She took a deep breath and held it, scanning his face. "Are you careful?"

"I am," he said. "I need to be. Getting someone pregnant isn't something I should..." His voice drifted off because, truth told, it had momentarily occurred to him to try to get Bella pregnant so that they'd be bound to one another for life. "Are you on the pill?"

She shook her head. "No."

"Shit," he sighed, rolling onto his back and throwing his arm over his eyes.

He felt her move, heard her rustling around on the blanket for a moment before she lay back down beside him, placing something on his chest.

Moving his arms, he looked down to see a square foil packet shining in the moonlight. He reached for it, propping himself on his side and looking down at her with wonder. "You brought one?"

She shrugged lightly, sitting up and taking it from his fingers. She tore it open with her teeth, which was just about the sexiest fucking thing Nico had ever seen in his life.

"I knew what I wanted."

Breathing in deeply, his cock throbbing for her touch, he was rewarded with her fingers wrapping around the base as she slipped the condom over his erection.

Unable to wait any longer to bury himself inside of her, he flipped her to her back, smiling down at her, finding her lips with his as he guided himself into her sex. Sliding inside as slowly as possible, he covered her mouth with his, stealing her breath as he broke through her virgin barrier.

She whimpered in pain, and it clutched at his heart.

"Are you okay?" he panted, deeply imbedded within her but perfectly still though the walls of her pussy throbbed around him.

"Give me a second," she answered breathlessly, her chest rising and falling quickly.

"Bella," he groaned, looking into her eyes as beads of sweat broke out across his forehead. "I love you."

She raised her legs experimentally, just a little, then a little more, until she was cradling his hips between hers. "I love you too."

And then he moved within her, pulling out then thrusting back inside, cradling her face as his body pumped into hers, loving the way she moaned as he moved faster, feeling the gathering in his balls, which tightened with every push. And Bella's body—*Dio*, for the rest of his life, he'd remember the way they fit together, the tightness of her sheath, the way she clung to him, panting into his ear, her sweet breath falling against his straining neck in puffs as her legs locked behind his back.

"I wish…," he grated out. "I wish, I wish…*O Dio, Bella, vorrei avervi sempre accanto a me!" I wish I could have you always by my side!*

"*Anch'io,*" she panted. *Me too.* "*Amami, Nico…amami…amami…amami…*"

Her words—*love me…love me…love me…love me*—were a litany of longing, of truth, of everything that he wished he could have. They tipped him over the edge of passion, and he found his release, crying out his own truth as he came inside of her:

"*Ti amo, mia cara Bella! Per sempre.*"
I love you, my darling Bella. Forever.

***

They slept for a while after making love, and when they awoke, it was much later—the sky almost black but for the full moon and brightest stars. For a while, rolled up in the blanket together, they stayed naked, sipping wine and snacking on cheese. Had Bella thought to bring a second condom, they would have made love a second time, but without it, they stared into one another's eyes for hours, their bodies flush against each other, holding one another tightly, kissing at will. As the seconds ticked by, though, their smiles were less brave, their hearts ever more heavy.

When the first light of dawn started brightening the sky, she felt a kind of panic seize her heart, but she pushed it aside, wiggling from their cozy cocoon and reaching for her bra and panties.

"You're getting ready to leave," he said softly from behind her, his voice heartbroken.

"It's time," she answered, clasping her bra. She stood up and picked up her dress, pulling it over her head. "I've stayed much longer than I should have."

"It's not light yet," he said.

"It will be. Very soon."

She gathered her thick black hair at the nape of her neck and bound it into a quick bun. She didn't want to cry—she didn't want Nico's last memories of her to be watching her cry—but her eyes had already started to burn, and she felt the warm wetness slip down her cheeks.

It had been the most beautiful night of her life. She wasn't ready to say good-bye. Turning around, she looked down at Nico, still partially covered with the blanket, gazing up at her with glistening eyes of his own. He braced his palm on the floor as though about to stand.

"Don't get up," she said quickly, kneeling down beside him.

"I hate this," he said, reaching for her cheek.

She leaned into his touch, closing her eyes, then forcing them open. "Don't hate it. Thirty minutes of wonderful, remember? We had a whole week."

"I'll live on it, Bella," he told her, "for the rest of my life."

She shook her head. "No, I don't want that. I want you to be happy."

"That feels impossible right now."

"Promise me you'll try."

His eyes shuttered closed as tears escaped, sliding slowly down his cheek. "I'll try."

She reached up to wipe away her tears, then leaned down to kiss him. It would be their last kiss, so she tried to notice every ridge of his lips, the way he sounded as he breathed in, the way he smelled—a mix of him and her—the way his hand felt against her face.

Drawing away, she swallowed a sob and somehow managed to say, "Be happy."

He covered his face with his hands, and she stood quickly, running across the roof to the stairwell door before she allowed herself to cry.

She walked quickly down the hall to the elevator, pressed the button for the thirty-second floor, and stepped out of the elevator to the glass doors of the salon. Taking the key from her pocket, she unlocked the doors and slipped inside, beelining through the dark space to the staff bathroom, where she sat down on the toilet and wept.

It was so blisteringly unfair that she should meet the love of her life and have to lose him. Just like Madame.

Madame.

She needed to get home before Madame, who was an occasional early riser, woke up.

Splashing her face with cold water, she straightened her dress, fashioned her long hair into a braid, and then left the salon and headed downstairs. As she pulled her key from her dress pocket, however, the door opened, and there, in the doorway, stood Madame.

"I warned you," she said, holding out Bella's passport to her.

"Please," whispered Bella, taking the little red book from Madame's fingers.

"I saw you," said Madame, crossing her arms over her chest and blocking the doorway. A mean smile tilted her lips. "Spreading your legs on the roof. I believe I have a picture on my phone if you want to see it."

Bella stared at her in shock and disgust, refusing to answer.

"Who was he?"

Clenching her jaw, Bella lifted her chin, looking Helga Gothel straight in the eyes. "I'm sorry."

"It's too late. You're out. I'll give you half an hour to get your—"

"I'm *not* sorry about last night," she said, her voice sure and strong. "I'm sorry he didn't love you."

Madame's eyes narrowed. "I don't know what you're—"

"But if you were as miserable *then* as you are *now*," she continued, "he made the right choice when he picked my mother."

"Karin stole him from me!" Madame Gothel exclaimed, her face red with fury. "He loved me first!"

Bella thought about her parents, about the way her father looked at her mother, about the way she tousled his jet-black hair, sighing with happiness.

"He loved her *better*," said Bella quietly, sidling past her godmother so she could go pack up her things,

She closed the door to her bedroom and pulled a suitcase from beneath her bed. She didn't have much—some clothes and toiletries, a few books, some framed pictures, and some jewelry that had been her mother's. Anything else she could replace once she got home.

Home.

Her heart ached with the goodness of it.

Taking the little change purse from her top drawer, she counted out her tips. Four hundred and sixty-two dollars. She doubted it would be enough for a plane ticket home. Sitting down on her bed, she looked at herself in the mirror over the dresser, at her father's jet-black hair that cascaded down her back to rest on the bed behind her.

And suddenly she knew exactly how she would get home.

CHAPTER 8
One Week Later

"*Bella, devi uscire con noi una sera*," said her coworker, Ilsa, using a broom to sweep the hair cuttings from around her styling chair. *You have to come out with us one night.*

"*Sì!*" cried Tia, who looked up from holding the dustpan for her cousin, Ilsa. "*Dai vieni con noi, sul serio. Al meno per un po'?*" *Come on out with us, girl! Just for a little?*

Bella put the two combs in her hand into the sterilizing solution, then gathered a handful of pins into her palm and shoved them into a drawer.

"*Non questa sera*," she said. *Not tonight.*

"You're too sad!" said Tia, hopping up to dump the contents of the dustpan into the trash. "You were never like this before going to America!"

Ilsa nodded in agreement. "You're breaking our hearts, Bella."

Since returning home to Bellinzona a week ago, Bella had been lovingly welcomed back by school friends who hadn't forgotten her. Indeed, Ilsa and Tia Bonasco, with whom Bella had grown up, had even helped her get a job here at Salone Rosa.

"I just…" She sighed, thinking of Nico's face and feeling her heart clench with agony. "I miss someone."

"But there are plenty of *someones* going to *La Fabrique* tonight!" insisted Ilsa. "And one of *those* someone's could be a *new* someone for you!"

Tia snorted at her cousin. "You're ridiculous, you know that?"

Smiling at her friends, Bella shook her head. "Soon, I promise. But for now? I think I'll just head home and relax."

"Home!" scoffed Ilsa. "A room! A very dreary room! You should come and stay with us."

Bella had earned $3,000 selling her hair, which had bought her an $800 one-way plane ticket home, and she'd taken a taxi straight to the Bellinzona Youth Hostel, where she'd lucked out in reserving a single room for two weeks.

Meanwhile, she'd also found an apartment to rent on Via Ghiringelli, but she couldn't move in until July 1...which was fine with Bella. While she was living at the hostel, she'd nurse her broken heart, but next week when she moved into her new apartment, she intended to start a new life that didn't include breath-stealing memories of a certain Italian prince.

"You two share a bed as it is," noted Bella. "Besides, my new place will be ready in a week."

"So you're just going to go home and weep some more?" asked Tia.

"No. I'm going to drink a few glasses of decent wine and watch the sunset before I get a good night's sleep."

"*Santa Bella* will be ready for church in the morning," said Ilsa, putting the broom away, "and we'll just be stumbling home."

"Come on," said Tia, putting her arm around Bella's shoulders as she withdrew the key to the salon from her pocket. "We're catching the bus. We'll walk you halfway to the hostel."

Her friends buzzed merrily about their Saturday-night plans as they walked with Bella, kissing her good-bye at the intersection of Via Dogana and Via Lugano, where they could catch a bus, then a train, north to *La Fabrique* nightclub in Castellone.

Bella waved good-bye to them, strolling through the piazza for Via Nocca, looking up at the castle on the hill and the mountains beyond and trying to feel grateful to be home. She was happy to be away from Madame Gothel, out from under her unkind keeping. She didn't miss the New York Metro Tower Hotel or any of the employees at the hotel with whom she'd worked for a handful of years.

But she missed Nico.

So badly, and with such a profound and constant yearning, sometimes she wasn't sure how she'd survive it.

Most nights she cried herself to sleep, remembering the tenderness of his caresses and the gentle sound of his trembling voice in her ear: *Ti amo, mia cara Bella! Per sempre.*

But she and Nico *hadn't* shared a forever love, just a breathless week of wonderful that she wished could have been more.

She kicked a pebble in her path, taking a ragged breath as she crossed her arms over her chest.

You were a fling, Bella, and so was he. A sweet summer fling. Let it be enough. Not all girls can look back and say that once upon a time they made love to a prince under a starry sky...

And yet she wasn't comforted by the thought. Maybe because she hadn't been making love to a prince; she'd been making love to Nico, and she missed him with every breath, every beat of her aching heart.

As she walked up to the gorgeous old villa that had been transformed into a youth hostel in 2002, she ran her fingers through her close-cropped hair, still trying to get used to it. She took a deep breath, wishing she could remember what kind of wine she'd stashed in the back of her closet. She'd purchased several bottles and was steadily plowing through them each evening in the hostel's courtyard, sitting alone in a wooden lounge chair by an ancient fountain until she was just drunk enough to fall into bed and have a cry before falling mercifully to sleep.

A good Merlot, I think. Or was it a—

"Bella."

She froze in her tracks, clenching her eyes closed and balling her fingers into fists by her sides.

It wasn't the first time it had happened this week—hearing his voice like she hadn't left him in New York without a forwarding address or word of any kind—but it was the cruelest of the tricks her mind played.

Except...

Except this time, someone reached for her right hand and was gently unfurling her fingers.

"Cara Bella. Ti prego...guardarmi." Darling Bella. Please...look at me.

She felt his breath on her lips, felt the warmth of his body near hers, but she feared that if she opened her eyes, the beautiful illusion would disappear.

"You look so different," he whispered close to her ear. *"Quasi non ti reconoscevo." I almost didn't recognize you.*

The Nico she left in New York wouldn't know anything about her cutting her hair…which meant…which meant…he was real!

With trembling fingers, she reached up to touch his face, sobbing as she opened her eyes to find him standing in front of her.

"Nico," she managed to whisper as her eyes traced the lines of his beloved face. There were circles under his eyes, his hair was messy, and his beard was thicker, but it was him. It was Nico De'Medici, her lost love, and he was somehow here with her in Bellinzona. *"Tu sei qui." You're here.*

"*Mi dispiace tantissimo, amore mio*," he murmured, pulling her into his arms. *I'm so sorry, my love.*

"For what?"

Tears trailed down her cheeks as she reached up to wind her arms around his neck, laying her cheek against his chest and inhaling the familiar scent of Acqua Nobile.

"For letting you go." She sobbed softly, clutching him tighter as he continued: "As soon as you left the roof, I knew I was making a mistake to let you say good-bye to me. I got dressed, cleaned up, and went back to my room to change. By the time I got to your apartment, you were gone, and that witch—your goddamned godmother—told me she'd kicked you out. I was out of my mind with worry! I had no idea where you'd gone, Bella. Where did you go?"

"To Brooklyn. I found a place that would buy my hair," she sobbed. "I sold it to come home."

He drew back, reaching for her cheeks, his fingertips touching the feathered layers of her cropped cut and his eyes glistening with tears. "You're so beautiful, Bella. So beautiful."

"I look different," she said, feeling a moment of insecurity.

"You look like my Bella," he said, brushing her lips with his.

"How did you find me?" she asked.

"I remembered you wanted to come home. I knew you were from Ticino…"

She nodded, smiling at him through her tears.

"…but I didn't know where. I left New York on Monday night for Lugano. I tried to think about where you'd be, where you'd go. I knew you didn't have money, so I checked at small hotels, but then it occurred to me that you might stay at an *osteria* for a little while to save money. You weren't in Lugano, so I tried the one in Locarno on Thursday. No again, but they were kind enough to call here, to ask if there was a Bella Capelli checked in." A tear slipped from his eye. "And you were here."

She reached up and swiped the tear away, cupping his cheek. His face was haggard and drawn, as sad and tired as hers. "You found me."

"I wasn't sure you'd want to see me."

"I need to know," she said. "Are you marrying her? Princess Elena?"

He shook his head. "No, Bella."

"You broke it off?" He didn't answer her right away and her heart lurched. "But your families. Your parents. The princess. *Dio, Nico!* Your two countries! I can't be the reason that—"

"Bella! Bella," he said, stopping her words with a sweet kiss, then resting his forehead against hers. "Let me tell you what happened. It's…well, it was sort of perfect. *La risposta ad una preghiera.*" *The answer to a prayer.*

"Tell me!" she insisted, her voice breathless with anticipation.

"She met someone else in Africa." He drew back and grinned at her, his eyes sparkling with happiness. "A doctor. From Sweden."

Bella let go of the breath she was holding, giggling as her eyes filled with more tears. "A doctor? Are you serious?"

"From Doctors Without Borders." He nodded, his eyes tracing her face as though memorizing it, as though recording it so that he could keep its image safe forever. "Someone who shares the same passion she does."

"*La risposta ad una preghiera.* Yes." She took a deep breath and sighed. "I'm so glad you didn't hurt her."

His eyes narrowed and he murmured, "But I would have."

"What do you mean?" she asked.

"I would have hurt her, walked away from her, *run* away from her…if that's what it would have taken to get to you. I'd already decided on that roof that I couldn't live without you…that my title, my family, Elena—*all of it* was expendable.

All that mattered was you." He rested his forehead on hers again. "You made me promise that I'd try to be happy. But Bella…I can't be happy without you. I wouldn't have proposed. I couldn't have possibly married her when I am totally in love with you."

"Nico…," she sobbed, her lips frantically searching for his and covering them with little kisses of pure happiness. *"Ti amo per sempre." I love you forever.*

"Ti amaró ancho per sempre, Bella." I'll also love you forever, Bella.

He held her tightly for a long while, rubbing her back as the sun started to set behind Montebello Castle on the hill behind them. It was almost as though they had to absorb it, trust it, believe that they were together again…and this time, it was forever.

When she leaned back to look at him, she couldn't help sighing with happiness, the same way her mother used to. "Are you really here?"

"I'm really here, *cara* Bella."

"And we don't have to say good-bye?"

"We have all the time in the world." She threw her arms around his neck, and he hugged her tightly. He whispered in her ear, "But we do have one little problem."

"What?"

"Any chance you'd take me on as a roommate?" he asked. "I have nowhere to stay in Bellinzona and I'd really *like* to stay with Bella."

She chuckled softly. "I have a twin bed if you don't mind sharing."

"I definitely don't mind sharing," he said with a wolfish grin. "It'll remind me of our blanket on the roof."

"I loved that blanket on the roof," she said wistfully.

"Me too," he said, kissing the tip of her nose. "Though it does seem like a raw deal for you, *cara* Bella. You fell in love with a prince…but I'm afraid a prince without a fortune isn't worth very much."

"To whom? To *me*, Nico De'Medici, you're everything. *Everything*," she said again, bathing in the love shining from his eyes and knowing the same was brightening hers. "Not to mention, you fell in love with a girl who had long, beautiful hair. Sure you still want me now?"

"Now and forever. I'm positive, Bella Capelli," he said softly, threading his fingers through the short jet-black strands as he drew her face to his to kiss her. "I didn't fall in love with your hair, *cara mia*. I fell in love with your heart."

The End

Thank you so much for reading Bella and Nico's short, sweet story. Find me on Amazon for more fairytale romances!

--Katy
xoxoxo

*****

As with all of my fairytales, 10% of the net royalties on paperback and e-book sales of this book during December 2017 will be donated to Lock of Love.

Locks of Love is a public non-profit organization that provides hairpieces to financially disadvantaged children under the age of 21 suffering from long-term medical hair loss from any diagnosis.

Learn more about Locks of Love (or make your own hair or monetary donation!) here:
http://www.locksoflove.org/

The Vixen and the Vet
2015 RITA® Finalist
2015 Winner, The Kindle Book Awards
(inspired by Beauty & the Beast)

Never Let You Go
(inspired by Hansel & Gretel)

Ginger's Heart
(inspired by Little Red Riding Hood)

Dark Sexy Knight
2017 Finalist, The Kindle Book Awards
(inspired by Camelot)

Don't Speak
2017 Silver Medalist, International Book Awards
(inspired by The Little Mermaid)

Shear Heaven
(inspired by Rapunzel)

At First Sight
(inspired by Aladdin)

Love Is Never Lost
(inspired by Rip Van Winkle)

For announcements about upcoming
a m o d e r n f a i r y t a l e
releases, be sure to sign up for Katy's newsletter at
http://www.katyregnery.com!

ALSO AVAILABLE
from Katy Regnery

a modern fairytale
(A collection)

The Vixen and the Vet
Never Let You Go
Ginger's Heart
Dark Sexy Knight
Don't Speak
Shear Heaven
At First Sight
Love is Never Lost

THE BLUEBERRY LANE SERIES

THE ENGLISH BROTHERS
(Blueberry Lane Books #1–7)

Breaking Up with Barrett
Falling for Fitz
Anyone but Alex
Seduced by Stratton
Wild about Weston
Kiss Me Kate
Marrying Mr. English

THE WINSLOW BROTHERS
(Blueberry Lane Books #8–11)

Bidding on Brooks
Proposing to Preston
Crazy about Cameron
Campaigning for Christopher

THE ROUSSEAUS
(Blueberry Lane Books #12–14)

Jonquils for Jax
Marry Me Mad
J.C. and the Bijoux Jolis

THE STORY SISTERS
(Blueberry Lane Books #15–17)

The Bohemian and the Businessman
The Director and Don Juan
Countdown to Midnight

THE SUMMERHAVEN SERIES

Fighting Irish
Smiling Irish
Loving Irish
Catching Irish

THE ARRANGED DUO

Arrange Me
Arrange Us

ODDS ARE GOOD SERIES

Single in Sitka
Nome-o Seeks Juliet
A Fairbanks Affair
My Valdez Valentine

STAND-ALONE BOOKS:

After We Break
(a stand-alone second-chance romance)

Braveheart
(a stand-alone suspenseful romance)

Frosted
(a stand-alone romance novella for mature readers)

Unloved, a love story
(a stand-alone suspenseful romance)

Under the sweet-romance pen name
Katy Paige

THE LINDSTROMS

Proxy Bride
Missy's Wish
Sweet Hearts
Choose Me
Virtually Mine
Unforgettable You

Under the paranormal pen name
K. P. Kelley

It's You, Book 1
It's You, Book 2

Under the YA pen name
Callie Henry

A Date for Hannah

ABOUT THE AUTHOR

New York Times and *USA Today* **bestselling author Katy Regnery** started her writing career by enrolling in a short story class in January 2012. One year later, she signed her first contract, and Katy's first novel was published in September 2013.

Over fifty books and three RITA® nominations later, Katy claims authorship of the multititled Blueberry Lane series, the A Modern Fairytale collection, the Summerhaven series, the Arranged duo, and several other stand-alone romances, including the critically acclaimed mainstream fiction novel *Unloved, a love story*.

Katy's books are available in English, French, German, Hebrew, Italian, Polish, Portuguese, and Turkish.

Check out Katy's Website here:
http://www.katyregnery.com
Sign up for Katy's newsletter today:
http://shorturl.at/aoCU3

www.ingramcontent.com/pod-product-compliance
Lightning Source LLC
Chambersburg PA
CBHW051308170626
46809CB00004B/1801